Gum and Ghouls

A WITCHY CANDY SHOP MYSTERY BOOK 3

NYX HALLIWELL

Beach
Path
Publishing

A house of illusions,
a cloak of disguise,
a web of enchantments,
woven with lies.
To break the spell,
to shatter the night,
the candy witch must follow whispers of starlight.
As her prophecy unfolds in a frightful embrace,
the faerytale princess bound by grace,
shall unearth the secrets in the light's revealing glow,
and Ever After's magic once more shall grow.

Chapter One

Bam, bam, bam.

The knocking jars me from sleep. Lightning flashes outside my second-floor bedroom window, and thunder rolls on its heels. Another rainstorm this late in the fall?

My feet hit the floor, and I jerk them back up. The wooden planks feel like slabs of ice.

Bam, bam, bam!

Who is out in this weather? And what creep is banging on the downstairs door of my candy shop at this too-early-in-the-morning o'clock?

Braving the chill, I flip on my dragon lamp, retrieve my robe, and locate my slippers. My eyes are blurry as I shuffle down the stairs and into the back room of the shop. Flicking on more lights, I grab a handful of coffee-flavored candies and pop one in my mouth. Instant calm and alertness hit my system from the sugar coating and the mix of espresso, cream, and vanilla.

Rain slides down the large glass panes of the display windows, and a hulking figure looms in the doorway. My magic instantly assesses if he is friend or foe—my gargoyle pendant, Onyx, lying against my collarbone, flares hot and then cools again instantly.

Interesting. My guardian can't decide.

This makes me even more wary. The size of the figure suggests a man, but the realm I come from has its share of sizable creatures, including trolls and good old giants. As I make my way across the tiled floor, I scan what I can see of the being from head to toe. The next flash of lightning shows that he's wearing a long trench coat, dark with rain and stained with mud. The hood is drawn up, and his features are obscured. The tip of a crossbow peeks over his massive shoulder.

Marlena, my godmother, rushes up behind me. She's also pulled on a robe and slippers, her salt and pepper curls piled on top of her head. "Who is that?"

The man cups his hands around his eyes and squints through the fogged-up glass door. He wipes away the condensation as he does, and my breath catches. Our eyes meet through the glass, and I step back, colliding with Marlena. "It can't be. "

But it is. He tosses off the hood, grins, and waves.

"Oh, dragon's blood," my godmother huffs, realizing who our guest is. "This can't be good."

Swallowing my desire to run screaming the other way, I do what any faerytale princess worth her salt would—invoke my magic to protect us, pop another candy, and open the door.

Wind buffets me, bringing icy rain with it. "Hansel?" I peek around his hulking body for his counterpart, but Gretel is nowhere in sight. "What are you doing here?"

He scoops me up in a bear hug, soaking my clothes, and another rumble of thunder drowns out my shocked cry.

"Princess Ambrosia!" He squeezes the air from my lungs. "It's good to set eyes on you!"

"It's Seraphina now," I tell him, pulling him inside. I make him remove his wet overcoat in the back room and hang it near the register to dry. Marlena brews tea, and we gather around the small table where she and I regularly take breaks during our busy days.

"'Tis a pretty name," Hansel says, his Ever After accent thick, "but why do you not use your given one?"

I've missed him, and I smile at his handsome face. I wish we hadn't parted the way we did. "In this realm, I must keep a low profile. Humans may love faerytales, but they don't believe they're real. Same goes for royalty."

"What in magic's name are you doing in this land?" Marlena inquires, eyeing Dradus, the crossbow Hansel insists on keeping strapped to his back. He's always been gifted with air elemental magic, and birds and other winged creatures adore him. His backup magic is earth, the same as his sister. "Where is Gretel?"

His body obscures the chair, and the slightly cracked teacup looks like a doll's in his hand. "Missing. I've come to find her and return her home."

I drop into the other chair and offer him a muffin of figs and chocolate. Gretel was one of my closest friends. I am distressed to hear such news. "Missing?"

"Aye. Two passings of the full moon now. The queen believes she has run away with a royal piece of jewelry. Your mother has placed a reward on my sister's fool head. I must find her before the hunters do."

Gretel is anything but a fool. Marlena and I exchange a guarded glance. We have my mother's royal brooch, which must be what the Queen is looking for. One of my enemies in this land possessed it, and I know Gretel to be innocent of such a crime. "Why would the Queen believe such a thing?"

"After you were banished, Gretel was inconsolable. The Queen wished to relieve her grief by exulting her above all of us at the guard." It is of the highest order to be part of the Royal Soldier Guard in Ever After. They are tasked with protecting the royal family and hunting down evil creatures sent from the Black Heart Court. "Your mother often placed the pin on Gretel's uniform so all would know she was Her Majesty's emissary. No harm was to be done to her, or it was..." He makes a slicing motion across his throat with his thumbnail. "She was supposed to be on a top-secret mission—she would not tell me the details. Then she disappeared. I fear she ran away from the kingdom, taking the brooch with her. I hoped I might find her here with you."

"Me?" While my friend had a knack for adventure, I doubt she would defy my mother and visit me, an Outcast accused of murder. "We have not seen her, but I assure you she no longer possesses the Queen's jewelry."

He eats his muffin in three bites. "How do you know?"

In my tiny office, I snag the brooch from its hiding spot. The crystals embedded in it glow magically upon my touch. I return to show it to him. "Because I have it."

His dark eyes round. He draws back. "Princess, that is treason. You are—"

"Banished, yes, I'm quite aware of that, Hansel."

"By the kingdom, how did you come by it?"

Our current houseguest picks that moment to make an appearance. She must have been drawn by the noise and his voice. She had—perhaps still has—a weakness for the big oaf. "Hansel?" Izzy says on a yawn.

At the sight of the Black Heart Court princess he believes

dead, Hansel jumps to his feet and nearly takes out the table. The teapot and cups bang against each other, slopping liquid onto the napkins. "You!" He points an accusatory finger at Izzy, knocking his chair over. His horrified gaze flicks to me, and then he reaches for his weapon. "Look out!"

"No!" I lunge for the crossbow, slapping down the arrow he's knocked with his air magic. The tip pierces the hem of my robe and embeds itself in the flooring. "It's not what you think."

"Not what I think?" He glowers as I yank the arrow free and examine my torn garment. "She tried to kill us, and she is..." He scans Izzy from the top of her black hair to her bare feet.

"Dead? Surprise!" Izzy's forehead creases, yet I see her struggle not to throw her arms around him. Once, we were all the best of friends, and her memory still exists in that time. "I was cursed, Hansel."

I hand him the arrow, glad it didn't sink itself into my foot. He often coats them with a paralyzing agent so that even if one of the handmade things doesn't kill you instantly, you are rendered immobile so he can interrogate you or finish the job himself. "She doesn't remember what happened," I explain. "There are forces at work here, and if Gretel is missing, she may be caught up in them, as well."

He continues to stare at Izzy as he speaks to me. "What have you done, Ambrosia? Raised the dead?"

The back door crashes open and a dark figure rushes in, shoving Izzy out of the way in order to reach me. He grabs me by both arms, his handsome face masked with concern. His vampyre magic rolls over me in a wave. "Princess, are you all right?"

Speaking of raising the dead. "Torren." My fingers itch to

wipe the raindrops from the master vampyre's long, dark lashes. "What are you doing?"

"I sensed your distress." His deep voice oozes concern in a sexy, melted chocolate way. He notices the rip in my robe. "You're hurt."

"No," I say, a little too breathy.

"But you *are* in danger."

Hansel raises his crossbow. "Only from the likes of you, nightwalker."

"No!" I cry, but the arrow is loosed and zings through the air.

Without taking his beautiful eyes off me, Torren snags it before it can plunge into his temple. Even with only one hand, he easily snaps the arrow in half, and it clatters to the floor at my feet.

"What bloody sorcery is this?" Hansel roars.

"Enough!" My godmother's voice rattles the rafters as though she is an equal to the thunder outside. She is. "Put that thing away this instant, Hansel, before I shove it up—"

"Marlena!" I draw Torren a step away from my old friend. "Hansel, meet Torren. Torren, Hansel." The two males stare each other down, neither speaking, until I'm ready to yell at them as well. "Torren is a good friend," I tell Hansel. "Torren, Hansel is also my friend. He's come looking for his missing sister."

Hansel narrows his eyes. "What are you to Princess Ambrosia?"

"Seraphina," I correct. "I don't use that name here, remember?"

Torren lifts a brow and glances at me. "Hansel, the faerytale character?"

"The very one," I say with a sigh.

Torren appraises him again but speaks to me. "Did he shoot you?"

"I would never," Hansel growls. "And I'll have you know, I am no character in a silly faerytale. She is the crown princess. I am sworn to protect her."

I should remove Torren's hand from my waist; it's warm and comforting, sending tingles to certain parts of my anatomy. I leave it there. "Hansel is in the Royal Guard. And this,"—I run my finger over the torn material—"is my fault. He was startled by Izzy's appearance, and I interceded. No harm done."

Izzy spreads her hands imploringly at Hansel. "Ambrosia— I mean, Seraphina—has told me what happened, yet I swear on the very Realm of the Queen, I have no memory of any such deed. I would never harm you or Gretel. You are my friends."

Hansel flicks his gaze to me. "Is it true? She remembers not what she did?"

The storm is slacking off, the pale gray bars of sunrise illuminating the front windows. I need to get the morning's offerings in the oven, or I'll have unhappy customers at opening time. "We believe she's been placed under a spell. Possibly, all of us were. I haven't ascertained the why or by whom." I have my theories but no solid proof. Yet. I reach for Izzy and pull her close, smiling at her and rubbing her arm in a comforting gesture. "But I will, and then we will set all to rights with the Queen."

Izzy nods, a fierce spark in her focused gaze. The other three parties seem less sure.

"Hansel, go with Marlena and get cleaned up. Izzy and I will start baking. Torren, I will provide you with a photo of Gretel. Can you ask around and see if anyone has spotted her?" At his nod, I continue. "Good. Once Hansel doesn't look like a drowned rat and I have time to bring him up to speed, he'll join you. We'll reconvene after closing today and discuss our next move."

Hansel makes a face. "You want me to work with *him*? A nightwalker?"

I pin him with a glower. Because I'm the Queen's daughter and of the royal bloodline, I command fealty, Outcast or not. It shows in my eyes, and my tone vibrates with it. "He is your best hope of finding your sister, and you will treat him with respect. Now, do as I say."

All heads bow. "Yes, your majesty," they chorus.

Except for Torren. He quirks that brow again and offers a smile that might melt all my inhibitions about him.

Chapter Two

When the bell jingles, I look up from the chocolate truffles I'm arranging on a plastic tiered tray with hearts painted on the sides. I plaster on a smile, forcing my worries aside.

"Welcome." I offer the lovely older woman a sample. "Can I tempt you with a sample of Cinnamon Vanilla Popcorn? It's perfect for Valentine's Day."

She accepts and orders a pound of it to go along with cookies and scones. As I package her order, the sweet aromas of caramel, vanilla, and freshly baked pastries swirl through the shop, mingling with the cheerful chatter of customers browsing the shelves. Marlena passes me with a tray of still-warm candy apples, their shiny red shells glistening under the soft lights.

"Mm mm, I bet this is how the cottage made of sweets in Hansel and Gretel smelled," a little girl exclaims to her mother. I chuckle to myself—if only they knew the truth of that cottage and my friends.

Speaking of which.

I hand the woman her bag of goodies and ring up the sale.

"There you go—have a faerytale day!" The door chimes again as she heads out into the bustling sidewalks of Enchanted Haven.

In the brief lull between customers, my eyes flick to the calendar on the wall. The countdown to the Enchanted Heart Festival glitters in pink and red—only a few days away. I've been busy concocting love potion lollipops and heart-shaped healing honey drops for the celebration, but I fear this latest development with Gretel will interfere with my baking plans.

I can't help but wonder—not for the first time—if Queen Veramis has something to do with the curse we're under and now Gretel's disappearance. The Black Heart Court Queen's shadow looms over me, her motivations always murky and ominous. I shiver slightly despite the warmth of the shop. If she did take Gretel...what dastardly plan is she up to now? My hand tightens on the counter. No matter what, I won't stop until I uncover the truth. That's a solemn Candy Witch vow.

Marlena and I work tirelessly all day helping customers. Izzy stays in the back, baking and following my candy recipes. Near closing time that afternoon, we're out of most of our bakery goods, but we've restocked the candy jars.

Nothing eliminates my worries, however, not even a constant supply of butterscotch candies. The chime alerts me to new customers, snapping me out of my dark musings. Torren and Hansel stride in, the cheerful bell at odds with their grim expressions.

"Well, well, if it isn't my two favorite customers," I say, trying to bring some forced cheer to their arrival. "Looks like you could use a pick me up."

Torren's eyes meet mine, and their intensity makes my smile falter. "We've found no trace of her."

Hansel nods, his brow furrowed. "A day-long search and

not a single lead." He runs a hand through his hair, frustration evident in the tense set of his broad shoulders. "Perhaps I was wrong—Gretel is not here, and she has no desire to be found."

I step out from behind the counter, my flowery skirt swishing. "Oh, Hansel. I'm so sorry. I can't imagine how hard this must be." Impulsively, I reach out and squeeze his arm. "You know I'm here for you, right? Anything you need."

He gives me a strained smile. "Thanks. I just...I feel like I've failed her somehow. We were always so close. Why didn't she come to me with her plans?"

"We know too little to make assumptions," Torren interjects. He has a fierceness to him that I attribute to the special relationship he enjoys with his own sister. "We will find her, I swear it on my immortal soul, and then you can ask her your questions."

Despite the moment's seriousness, I can't help but tease him. "Careful, Torren. Oaths sworn on immortal souls pack quite a magical punch with those of us from Ever After."

The corner of his mouth twitches. "I'm well aware, but I mean every word."

A tingle runs through me at the conviction in his tone. "Well, all this grave vowing calls for some sustenance, I think. How about a Resilient Raspberry Truffle or two? Guaranteed to keep you going, no matter how hopeless the quest may seem."

As I reach for the candy, color out of the corner of my eye makes me turn sharply. "What is that?"

Hansel steps forward, a scrap of vibrant red fabric clutched in his fist. "We found this near the Witching Well."

My breath catches as I reach out to take it, my fingers brushing against Hansel's warm skin. I examine the scrap closely, my brows furrowing. The material is soft and finely woven, shot through with delicate golden threads that catch the light like stardust. "It looks like it could be from Gretel's cloak."

"I thought so, too, but it holds none of her magic."

"No, it's definitely hers," I murmur, my mind racing with possibilities. Why would a piece of her cloak be at the Witching Well? Has she been in Enchanted Haven, as Hansel suspected? The questions swirl inside me like a tempest.

Torren's presence is commanding even in the cozy confines of my shop. "It's said that the waters there hold powerful magic, capable of granting desires...or leading one astray."

I shoot him a sharp look. "Gretel's earth magic has always been woven into her clothes. Even if Hansel can't feel it, I know this fabric. It's hers."

"But the Well could be giving you what you seek—not what's true," he counters.

Hansel's jaw clenches, determination etched into every line of his face. "'Tis the only lead we have. If Ambro—Seraphina—believes it to be hers, we must follow it."

I nod, my grip tightening on the scrap of cloak. He's right. As much as I want to protect and shield him from the painful possibilities, I know we can't ignore this. Surely, I can concoct a candy that will keep the Well from misleading us if it is trying to do so. "We'll go to the Witching Well. Together. Like Hansel and Gretel, off on another adventure."

The ghost of a smile flickers across his face at my weak attempt at humor. "Let's hope this one has a sweet ending, yes?"

I tuck the fabric into my pocket, my heart beating an irregular rhythm. *What happened to you, Gretel? How is it you were here in town and I didn't know? Why didn't you find me?* "Give me a minute to create a candy to aid us. A bit of sugar, spice, and magic." That's the recipe for any good faerytale.

Torren clears his throat, a touch of impatience in his eyes. "Perhaps we should make haste before the trail grows colder than the graveyard."

"Right." I square my shoulders, feeling a flicker of hope amidst the worry. "I'll be right back."

As I bustle around the backroom, gathering enchanted ingredients and protective charms, I wonder again why my dear friend didn't reach out to me. Maybe she tried, but someone stopped her before she could.

Marlena is washing pans and trays. Tired from candy-making, Izzy has already retired to her bedroom. I show my godmother the scrap of fabric and explain where Torren and Hansel found it. That it could be a clue or it could be nothing. She wipes her hands on a dish towel and then sniffs the fabric. "You're sure," she says, her voice carrying a note of concern. "It's definitely Gretel's?"

I nod. "We're returning to the Well to look for other clues."

Marlena hums thoughtfully, her gaze distant. "You know, the locals claim it whispers and that it offers the ability to grant wishes...and to take them away." She fixes me with a mean-ingful look. "Might Gretel have gone to it for such a reason?"

True. I hadn't considered that. "It's worth investigating."

Marlena's expression is tinged with wisdom from centuries of experience. "You and I know that there's often a kernel of truth in even the most fanciful of stories. And when it comes to the safety of those we love..." She shrugs, the gesture saying more than words ever could.

If there's even a chance it could lead us to Gretel, I have to take it. "I suppose we're off to make a wish, then," I say, injecting a note of lightness into my tone.

Marlena chuckles. "Shall I bring Gunther, just in case? Enchanted Haven's magic has a way of twisting even the sweetest intentions."

I grin, feeling a rush of affection for my godmother. "Good thing I've got a few tricks up my sleeve, a pocketful of enchanted candies, and you and the others, just in case."

"Let me change," she says, "and I'll be right with you."

Izzy comes flying down the stairs, her voice tinged with excitement. "I'm coming, too. I won't be a bother."

I hesitate, but as I meet her eager gaze, I waver. She's been a true friend through thick and thin, and her unique perspective could offer insights. Plus, I hope some good might come from this and repair the damage between her and Hansel. Still, she's been through so much, and what if this hunt leads to something sinister about her mother? "Someone needs to keep an eye on the shop."

Her face falls, disappointment clouding her features. "I can't just sit here twiddling my thumbs while Gretel's out there, possibly in danger."

"Let her come," Hansel from behind me. He fingers his crossbow. "Helping us is the least she can do."

Allowing her to work with us may set his mind at ease. "Alright, alright," I relent, unable to suppress a smile at her delighted squeal. "But you have to promise to stick close and follow my lead. No wandering off or poking your nose where it doesn't belong, okay?"

Izzy nods, her wild mane of hair bouncing with the motion. "Cross my Black Heart heart."

I shake my head, laughing despite myself, as we all gather at the door. "Ready?" I ask, meeting the eyes of my companions.

They nod. The Witching Well awaits, and with it, the

potential of answers. Perhaps, if we're lucky, it will also grant a happy ending to this particular faerytale.

My emotions rise and fall as I walk next to Torren on the way there. Our partnership in solving mysteries has earned us a reputation with the town and a few assignments from Mayor Jo. "I guess we can consider this a new case, although I'm not sure this is one our good mayor will be interested in."

Torren scans the people we pass as if searching for Gretel in each of their faces. "Every day with you is an adventure."

A pleasant warmth blooms in my chest. Silly, I know. The familiar tingle of his magic dances across my skin, a comforting reminder of the power that flows through both of us.

As we make our way to the town center, a flicker of unease flares in the pit of my stomach. The Witching Well has always been a source of intrigue and mystery, even in a town where magic is as common as candy canes at Christmas.

I slip my hand into my coat pocket, my fingers brushing against the smooth surface of the candies I've tucked away there. The familiar shapes—a swirled lollipop, a star-shaped gummy, and a spherical jawbreaker—bring a small measure of comfort.

"I won't rest until we find my sister and bring her home," Hansel says as we pass the church.

Izzy, who's been uncharacteristically quiet, pipes up then. "We'll find her. And when we do, we'll celebrate with a batch of Seraphina's famous 'Happily Ever After' cupcakes."

Izzy's optimism is like a sugar rush for my soul. I square my shoulders and fix my gaze on the path ahead. Somewhere out there, Gretel needs us. And I won't stop until we've unraveled this mystery and brought her safely home.

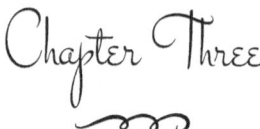

Chapter Three

The Witching Well beckons us forward, its ancient stones whispering secrets of countless wishes made. In the background, City Hall looms, and I expect Mayor Jo watches us from his office.

Our footsteps echo on the stone road, a rhythmic reminder of our urgent mission. My heart aches for Gretel, wondering where she could be and if she's all right. Did she leave Ever After because of me or something more dangerous?

Torren's cool fingers brush mine as he presses a gold coin into my palm. "Make a wish, Seraphina," he murmurs, his dark eyes glittering in the late afternoon sun. His magic wraps around me like a warm, well-worn blanket. I wish to curl up in it.

Closing my eyes, I feel the coin's weight, cool and promising. *Please*, I think, *give us a clue to find Gretel. Let her be safe.* That's two wishes, but I can't help it.

With a flick of my wrist, I send the coin spinning into the bubbling waters. The soft *plunk* as it hits the bottom seems too small, too meaningless.

"Do you think it worked?" Hansel asks.

I open my eyes, searching the Well's depths as if Gretel's location might be written in the ripples. "I hope so. If not, I will whip up a locator spell stronger than my triple fudge brownies."

Marlena quirks a brow. Locator spells aren't something I'm gifted at, and our magic sometimes worked oddly here, the simplest spells backfiring. Under the circumstances, I'm willing to risk it.

Torren's hand finds the small of my back, a comforting and distracting gesture. I can almost taste the magic on my tongue, as rich and complex as the dark chocolate truffles I arranged earlier today. But beneath it all, a current of unease swirls, bitter and frightening.

"What now?" Izzy asks, glancing at each of us. "Should we split up and search the town again? Or stick together?"

The answer doesn't come immediately, and I find myself wishing that finding Gretel was as simple as following a trail of candy through the forest. Enchanted Haven is no faerytale wood, and while most humans here don't realize they share the town with supernaturals, dark magic affects them as readily as it does us.

"The wisest move would be to separate into two groups," Torren says. "Hansel, Izzy, and Marlena, you take the west side of town. Seraphina and I will take the east."

The sharp click of heels catches my attention. Dr. Maude Trumball approaches, her white dentist jacket flapping in the breeze. "Well, well," she says, peering at us over her low-riding glasses. "What's *brewing* at the Witching Well today?" She seems to enjoy her pun. "Wishing for something special, Seraphina?"

I resist the urge to roll my eyes. "Our friend Gretel has gone missing. We're trying to find her. We believe she may have visited here." Reaching into my pocket, I pull out the red scrap of fabric. "We found this, which appears to have been torn from her favorite cloak."

Maude's stern expression softens a fraction as she examines the cloth. Her brow furrows, reminding me of the ridges on a peanut butter cup. "How curious," she murmurs. "You know, I saw something odd the other day that might be related."

My heart skips a beat. "What was it?"

"A stranger in a red cape." Her voice lowers as if sharing a secret. "I spotted her during my morning walk in Whimsy Park yesterday morning."

I exchange glances with my friends, a spark of hope igniting in my chest. Could this be a breadcrumb we're looking for?

"Dr. Trumball," I say, eager to follow it, "you might have just given us our first real clue. Thank you."

Maude looks surprised as if she's not used to being thanked. "Well," she says, straightening her coat, "I hope it helps. Is she...like you?"

Maude suspects that I'm more than what I seem. She's been exposed to several of my magical spells and seen the space between this realm and Ever After. I smile, placating. "She's special to us."

Puzzling it out, she gives a hesitant nod. "The strange thing was, this woman was talking to a tree. Enchanted Haven has its quirky personalities,"—she gives me a pointed look—"but that seemed...particularly peculiar."

"A tree?" Hansel is so eager he steps toward her, and she hurriedly backs away from his towering bulk. "Did you hear what she was saying?"

"I'm afraid not," Maude shakes her head, her tight bun barely moving. "I only caught a brief glimpse. One moment, she was there, and the next time I glanced her way, she was gone."

"She always loved trees," Izzy says.

As I mull over this new information, Maude's stern voice snaps me back to reality. "When are you going to stop avoiding your dental check-up?"

"Oh, you know me, Dr. Trumball. I'll get there soon." Not.

Maude narrows her eyes. "Make an appointment soon."

As she strides away, I can't help but think that facing a wicked witch might be less daunting than a dental exam with her.

As soon as Maude's out of earshot, Torren clears his throat. "Mayor Jo tasked me with investigating some strange magical disturbances in Whimsy Park."

My candy-coated world suddenly feels a bit less sweet. "I thought we were partners. Why didn't you say anything?"

"You've been busy preparing for the Valentine's Day festival. I didn't mention it because, well, I hadn't found anything concrete yet. There was no point in causing you undo worry or stress."

I bite back a retort—it was courtesy, nothing more, and I should appreciate his kindness. "Do you think these disturbances are connected to Gretel's disappearance?"

Hansel pipes up, his standard soldier's stance softening a bit. "Gretel may have been investigating them, too. She always talks to trees when she needs information."

Izzy's eyes light up. "If we can figure out which tree it was, I might be able to discover what it shared with Gretel."

A plan begins to take shape in my mind. "Looks like we're off to see the wizard—or, in this case, a chatty tree in Whimsy Park."

My senses are on high alert, and as we enter the park, I can't shake the prickly sensation crawling up my neck. It's as if unseen eyes are following us, watching us from the shadows.

"Seraphina?" Torren's voice cuts through my paranoia. "Is everything alright?"

Is this how Little Red felt when the wolf was stalking her? I scan the area and see nothing. No glowing eyes or flashing fangs. "Besides the fact that there are at least fifty trees here, and we have no idea which one Gretel may have spoken to?"

"You seem on edge. Like you're expecting a gingerbread man to jump out and bite you."

He knows all about my gingerbread men and how I can make them come to life. I laugh, but it sounds hollow to my ears. "If you don't sense anything unusual, then no. It's just my overactive imagination. You know how it is—too much sugar, not enough sleep."

The path winds before us, the February chill crisp. Early spring flowers peek through the frosty ground, their pastel petals a stark contrast to the bare branches above. Towering trees line our way, their limbs swaying in the breeze.

A familiar figure emerges from the woods to our left. Cynric, our resident werewolf and reverend, bounds towards us with a curious wave. "If it isn't my favorite pack of trouble-makers," he grins. "What brings you to this neck of the woods?"

Torren motions him out of our way. "We're on a mission. Seraphina's friend, Gretel, has gone missing, and we have reason to believe she might have been here recently."

"Missing?" Cynric's playful demeanor shifts to concern. "How can I help?"

I introduce him to Hansel, and the two size each other up, but Hansel doesn't react to the shifter as he did to the vampyre.

"Actually, your nose might be just what we need," Hansel says. "Could you track Gretel's scent?"

"Say no more," Cynric nods, his nostrils already flaring. "I'd be happy to lend a paw—er, hand."

Hansel offers to shake, and Cynric accepts. "A pleasure," Hansel says, a hint of relief in his voice. "We are glad to have you join us."

With Cynric's keen senses along with Torren's and mine, surely we'll find another clue to Gretel's whereabouts.

As Cynric sniffs the air, I do, too. The sweet scent of the early spring blossoms mingles with the earthy aroma of damp soil. I send my magical feelers out but come up empty. I can't tell if Gretel was here or not. And still, that nagging feeling of being watched persists.

Torren hovers close, his tall frame casting a protective shadow. "Seraphina," he murmurs, his voice low and velvety, "what's really troubling you? I can sense there's more than just concern for Gretel."

I bite my lip, unsure how to explain the prickly feeling at the nape of my neck. "It's probably nothing."

Torren's dark eyes search mine, clearly not buying my dismissal.

"I should probably shift," Cynric says. "My wolf form is more acute."

I nod. "Let's spread out. Hansel, you go north with Cyn. Izzy, you and Marlena head east. Torren and I will continue this way. Keep your eyes peeled for anything unusual and your magic scanning for signs that Gretel used hers."

All magic leaves a trace. If we can catch the slightest hint of hers, we'll be able to track her. As our group fans across the park, Torren and I pass towering oaks and maples that stand like silent sentinels, their branches reaching toward the sky.

Clouds form and skitter overhead, blocking out the weakening sunlight.

It's like trying to find the prize in a box of crackerjacks—you know it's there, but it keeps slipping through your fingers. We walk one pathway after another, noting all the trees and bushes, most still skeletal from winter. We examine the children's playgound, look inside trash receptacles, and scan the park benches.

"Any luck?" I call to Cynric when he and Hansel are within earshot.

The giant wolf shakes his head, frustration evident in his twitching ears. He speaks around his fangs, making the words less distinctive but still understandable. It reminds me of a child talking while chewing on sticky taffy. "There's something, but it's faint. Like the scent of sugar on the wind from your shop when I'm at the church."

I nod, reminding myself that even the most complex recipes start with simple ingredients. We need to find our next clue, and the rest will surely follow.

As the path leads us into the heart of the park, the trees create a canopy, and shadows dance at the corners of my vision. Again, I can't shake that eerie feeling that we're being watched and not by the friendly woodland creatures that call this place home.

"Seraphina," Torren's voice cuts through my thoughts. "Have you seen a ghost?"

I have a penchant for spotting spirits, and they sometimes talk to me. A familiar one is Flower, who appears and disappears around town frequently. "Not a ghost." Or maybe it is. I peer at the shadows beyond the closest line of trees. "It's just a feeling, but—"

Marlena's voice rings out, interrupting us. "Over here, by the hedgerow! I think I've found something!"

We rush to her and Izzy, leaves crunching beneath our feet. As we approach, I spot something glinting in the grass, out of place.

Hansel kneels, his face grim as he picks up the object. A crow charm—it was Gretel's favorite. "It's hers," he says, his voice as rough as rock candy. "From her charm bracelet. She never takes that thing off."

"I gave her that charm," Izzy says, panic in her eyes when she meets my gaze.

My heart sinks. "I remember. Guess the Witching Well is granting my wish. We have a solid clue."

"Look at the hedgerow." Torren gestures to the damaged foliage. "These branches are snapped. There was a struggle here."

I swallow hard, the sweet taste of hope turning bitter in my mouth. "So Gretel was taken?"

Hansel's jaw clenches, his hand instinctively moving to his crossbow. "If someone's hurt my sister, they're going to wish they'd never set foot in Enchanted Haven."

"Keep your bow sheathed," Marlena commands, her tone firm. "Don't jump to conclusions. We don't know that, and perhaps Gretel was the aggressor."

Although Hansel blusters, I agree. "Marlena's right. She's part of the Queen's guard like you, Hansel. That could explain a lot if she was sent on a mission to track down a criminal or Outcast wanted by the realm. We need a plan. But first..." I turn back to Torren, my resolve hardening. "There's something I need to tell you all. I think we might be in more danger than we realized."

Chapter Four

"What is it?" Torren asks.

I lower my voice so it's barely above a whisper. "I think we're being—"

A searing heat against my collarbone cuts me off mid-sentence. My hand flies to Onyx, my gargoyle pendant. Its burn is a stark warning against my skin.

"Seraphina?" Torren's dark eyes lock onto mine, concern etched across his face. "What's wrong?"

Before I can answer, the ground beneath us rumbles like an angry giant's stomach. In a blink, thorny vines erupt from the moss-covered path, their emerald tendrils reaching for us with wicked intent.

"Sweet sugarplums!" I gasp, stumbling backward as a vine snags my sleeve. The thorn rakes across my skin, leaving a line of fire in its wake.

"Everyone, move!" Torren shouts.

My heart pounds as I fumble for the pouch of enchanted candies. The vines writhe and twist, their thorns glistening with an ominous sheen that would make even the most wicked of stepmothers jealous.

Torren shields me. "Use those wisely," he says, nodding at the candies

I'm grateful for his presence. "Time to show these vines that they've bitten off more than they can chew!" One thing's for sure—this mission has taken an unexpected turn. I toss a handful of magical gumballs into the air. "Hope you like dessert!" I shout at the encroaching vines.

The candies explode, transforming into a sticky, sweet barrier that stretches between us and our thorny menaces. The scent of bubblegum fills the air as the vines slam into the makeshift wall, their progress halted by the gooey concoction.

"Ingenious as always, Seraphina," Cynric says. "Your candies never cease to amaze."

"Let's just hope they hold long enough for us to—"

"Everyone, gather close," Hansel's deep voice cuts through the chaos. His amber eyes narrow with determination as he steps forward, the air around him humming with magical energy.

It sends ripples over my skin. "What are you up to, Hansel?"

He doesn't answer, instead raising his hands in a sweeping gesture. The ground beneath our feet trembles again, and for a moment, I fear the vines have broken through. But then, to my astonishment, the earth itself begins to rise around us and form a protective wall, shielding us from the relentless assault of the evil viney weapons.

The wall grows higher, solid and unyielding. It matches the determination in Hansel's eyes.

"Hansel, you're incredible," Izzy says, a bit out of breath.

He offers a small smile, his focus still on maintaining the

barrier. "Just doing my duty, Princess. Though I must admit, Seraphina's candy trick was quite impressive."

As we huddle within our newfound sanctuary, I contemplate what to do next. "Anyone up for a game of 'Guess Who's Trying to Kill Us'?"

The vines prove they're not ready to give up their twisted game, though. The thorny tendrils slither high into the air, weaving and twisting until they form words that chill me to my core.

"Turn...back...or," I read aloud, my voice shaking. "...die."

A shiver shakes me, but I've faced worse than some overgrown weeds with an attitude problem. "Well," I say, forcing a smile, "that sounds ridiculously dramatic."

Izzy giggles nervously beside me. "Maybe we should offer them some of your candied roses, Sera. Sweeten them up a bit?"

Her joke falls flat as she suddenly stumbles, her face draining of color. An odd sound comes from her throat.

"Izzy!" I cry out, reaching for her.

But Hansel is faster. He scoops Izzy into his arms before she can hit the ground. "She's been hit," he says, his voice tight with worry. "The thorns..."

I gasp as I see blood from several wounds on Izzy's arms and legs. The poison left behind is spreading visibly, dark tendrils creeping beneath her skin. She goes rigid and whimpers. My own arm pulses in sympathetic agony.

"Oh, Izzy," I whisper, my heart breaking at the sight of my friend in pain. "Don't worry, we'll fix this. I promise."

I turn my attention back to the remaining vines. They're still writhing and twisting, their thorns glinting menacingly in the setting sun's fading rays. "Marlena," I say, "think you and Gunther can give these overgrown weeds a trim?"

Her curls bounce as she nods. "With pleasure," she replies, her voice dripping with sarcasm. "Gunther's been itching for some action."

She wields her sword with the grace of a dancer and the precision of a master confectioner. Gunther slices through our attackers like they're nothing but spun sugar. The severed tendrils drop to the ground, writhing before slithering back into the soil.

As the last of the vines retreat, I take a moment to catch my breath. My mind is racing faster than Cinderella's pumpkin coach at midnight, full of questions about the warning we received. I exchange a worried glance with Marlena, her wise eyes reflecting my concerns.

Torren's smooth voice cuts through my thoughts. "That was quite the prickly situation. Perhaps I should heal your injuries before—"

"No!" I interrupt, feeling that same ominous presence creeping up the back of my neck. "We need to get to cover first. We're too exposed here."

"As you wish."

With him, Cynric, and Marlena forming a shield around us, I lead the charge back to The Candy Cauldron. The cobblestone streets of Enchanted Haven blur beneath my feet as we race against time and the poison.

"Hang in there, Izzy," I whisper, glancing at Hansel, cradling her. She's gone limp. His jaw is set, determination etched into every line of his face.

As we round the corner, the whimsical storefront of the shop comes into view. The bright gingerbread trim I just installed starkly contrasts with the gravity of our situation.

"Almost there," I pant, fumbling for my keys. My arm

burns hot, and I send as much healing magic as I can into it to slow the advance of the poison.

Torren sees how my fingers tremble and uses his magic to unlock the door, ushering me through first. "Your injury needs attention."

Inside, my shop's familiar warmth is a balm to my nervous system. But there's no time to savor it. "Not as much as Izzy's does." I direct Hansel upstairs to her bedroom, and we all follow.

He gently lays her on the bed, her wild mahogany hair fanning out on the pillow. My heart pinches at how small and vulnerable she looks.

"Stand back," Hansel commands. He places his hands on either side of Izzy's head, closing his eyes in concentration.

A soft, earthy glow emanates from his palms, seeping into Izzy's skin and flowing down over her torso and limbs. I watch, mesmerized, as the angry red lines of poison trailing up her arms begin to recede.

"It's working," I whisper, hardly daring to breathe.

Hansel nods, sweat beading on his brow. "The poison's retreat is slow, but aye, it is retreating."

I grip the bedpost, feeling faint. "Come on, Izzy," I murmur. "Don't go all Sleeping Beauty on us now. We need your sass and sparkle."

Torren grabs me by the arm and leads me to a chair, where I sink down. He examines my arm and then presses one of his hands over the wound.

Instant cooling magic calms the raging agony. I release an audible sigh. Cynric and Marlena join us, hovering in the doorway.

I'm jolted from my thoughts as Marlena sweeps in,

Gunther gleaming at her side. "Let Gunther take the poison," Marlena commands, offering the blade to Hansel.

He places Gunther's flat side against Izzy's stomach. The sword hums softly, its magic pulsing in rhythm with her labored breathing. I watch, fascinated, as dark wisps of poison begin to curl away from her, drawn into Gunther's blade.

"I didn't know you could do that," I mutter, unable to contain my awe.

Marlena's eyes crinkle with amusement. "I would think by now you knew all of my secrets. Just wait 'til you see the encore."

As if on cue, Torren accepts the sword from Marlena. His vampyre magic has halted the poison's spread in my body, and now he uses Gunther to extract it, giving a bit of a flourish as he bows when the blade is done. "Right as rain again, your Majesty."

"Show-off," I tease, trying to ignore the flutter in my stomach at his smoldering smile.

Leaving Hansel to watch over Izzy, the rest of us retreat downstairs. I busy myself at the counter. Marlena takes Gunther outside to neutralize the poison in the soil. "Time for some magical pick-me-ups," I announce, grabbing an assortment of leftover treats.

I'm so focused on arranging the platter of cookies that I nearly trip over Lady Wyndolynn as she weaves between my legs.

Watch it, sugar cube, her voice echoes in my mind. *I require sustenance, too.*

"Well, excuse me for being a little on edge after nearly being turned into vine food," I retort, scooping her into my arms.

She squirms in my embrace, her green eyes narrowing. *Put me down. I'm not your teddy bear.*

But I can't let go. Not yet. The consequences of everything that's happened crashes over me like a wave of molten caramel, and I bury my face in her soft fur, seeking comfort.

There, there. Lady Wyndolynn's mental voice softens. *You and your friends are fine. But if you don't let me go in the next three seconds, I'm using your leg as a scratching post.*

So much for sympathy. I set her down, only to find myself enveloped in a different, much taller embrace. Torren's arms wrap around me, solid and secure.

"You were magnificent out there," he murmurs, his breath tickling my ear.

I should step away and maintain that professional distance. But right now, at this moment, I can't bring myself to move. Instead, I lean into him, allowing myself a moment of sweetness amid our bitter situation.

Chapter Five

I watch as Marlena delicately cradles the cracked charm in her palm. The tiny crow figurine pulses and emits a soft caw. I can almost feel the protective earth magic radiating from it—Gretel's magic—but it wanes even as we stare at it.

Marlena eases her fingers around the edges. "This charm holds a powerful enchantment."

A soft groan draws my attention. Izzy stumbles into the room, her mahogany ringlets in disarray. Hansel hovers protectively behind her. "Easy there," he says gruffly.

"How are you feeling?" I ask her.

"Like I've been trampled by a herd of trolls." Her gaze falls on the charm in Marlena's hand. "It's truly hers?"

"Her magic is all over it," I confirm.

Izzy places a steadying hand on the worktable. "Gretel and I used to feed the crows in the Whispering Woods back home. They'd bring us tiny trinkets in return—shiny pebbles, bits of ribbon. That's why I gave her that charm."

Marlena sets it down, eyeing it cautiously. "Gretel, or someone, enchanted it. Any chance you know who or why? What the enchantment is for?"

She rubs her forehead. "Gretel said it would always connect us, no matter where we were, but I don't think she put a spell on it."

Could this be the key to finding our friend? "How exactly did she believe it connected you?"

"She claimed if she rubbed the charm, she could sense where I was." Her eyes widen. "Do you think it might work in reverse? If I hold it, can I sense where she is?"

Marlena makes a humming noise as she pokes at the crack. It makes that soft caw again, almost as if in pain. "Perhaps, but we must repair it first."

"Then do so," Hansel orders.

Marlena lifts a scolding brow. "We all wish to find her. Rudeness does none of us any good."

He dips his chin. "My apologies. I only wish to find her."

"As do we all," Izzy says, laying a hand on his arm.

"I've got just the thing," I announce, hurrying to one of my cabinets. The glass doors reflect the light as I swing them open, revealing rows of colorful jars filled with ingredients and my own creations. I pluck out a jar of gummy bears. "These little guys aren't just for snacking."

"Of course not." Izzy scrutinizes them. "What can they do?"

"A wide host of things," Torren mutters. When everyone looks his way, he shrugs. "During our investigations, Seraphina has used them quite liberally to assist us."

He's not a big fan of my candies, yet they have indeed been a valuable resource on several occasions. I tap the jar. "This particular batch is for magical repairs."

Carefully, I select three: red, blue, and golden. When I lay them on a piece of parchment near the charm, they pulse.

"Are they alive?" Hansel asks. "It looks as though their hearts are beating."

"Each has a heartbeat of sorts since they come from me," I explain. "Theirs beat in tune with my own. Let's see if they can work a bit of candy magic."

Izzy presses her hands together. "I love your magic, Sera."

As I pick up the red one, its sweet, berry scent reminds me of summer picnics in the palace gardens back in Ever After. I push the bittersweet memory aside and focus on the task at hand.

"Here goes nothing." I press it against the charm's crack as I command, "Candy, repair the break and make the charm whole again." It begins to melt, filling the air with the berry aroma and a hint of warm caramel. The liquid seeps into the crack, and the crow begins to glow.

"It's working!" Hansel says, leaning in for a closer look.

I nod, concentrating as I reach for the blue bear. "One down, two to go."

"It needs another?" Cynric asks. From the way he eyes the tiny candies, I know he's hungry and would be happy if there were leftovers he could eat.

I push a plate of the day's leftover cookies at him. "This will be more to your liking." To the others, I explain, "Each candy has a job—one to repair the crack, another to stabilize the repair, and the third to strengthen the charm's connection to Izzy."

I command the blue bear to commence with its job. As it melts, adding a layer of blueberry and coconut to the scented air, Hansel touches Izzy's arm, where a wound is healed but still pink. "Did you learn anything from the trees in the park?"

She fidgets with the hem of her shirt. "I...I don't know if I heard them correctly," she stammers.

I squeeze her hand. "It's okay. Just tell us what they said."

She draws a deep breath. "When I touched the oldest oak, it was like diving into a pool of memories. I wasn't only feeling the tree's bark under my fingers, I saw through its eyes. Freaky, right? Do you think I've lost my mind?"

Marlena snorts. "Nothing is too freaky in this group."

"Gretel saw what the trees did all the time," Hansel says.

"Yes, *Gretel* did." Izzy emphasizes her name. "She's an earth elemental, so it makes sense that she can do that. I'm from the Dark Heart Court, a shadow kingdom. That's not a talent we have. Honestly, I'm not sure what my talents are these days."

Torren comes to my side, addressing her with gentleness. "After what happened to you, your magic is suppressing itself, either because of the curse placed on you or because you're frightened of it. Either way, you are safe here, and when the curse is lifted, and you feel confident with your talents once more, they will surface."

At that moment, I love him. Not *love* love—at least not that I'm ready to admit—but the fact he's reassuring my friend means everything to me. "What did you see, Iz?"

Her eyes grow distant. "I saw my mother with the witch Cambria. They were having a hushed but animated conversation under the tree. It was as if the air around them was charged with dark magic, making the branches tremble."

Hansel narrows his eyes, his instincts clearly on high alert. "What were they saying?"

Izzy's voice drops to a whisper, her gaze still unfocused "It was about harnessing the power of the bubbling waters Mother said something about 'bending reality to her will.'"

My stomach drops. "The Witching Well."

"That doesn't sound at all ominous," Cynric says around the last bite of cookie. "What does it mean?"

Marlena drums her fingers on the table. "She's toying with the fabric of both our worlds."

A chill laces its way along my spine despite the warmth of my shop. "If Queen Veramis gains that kind of power, she could—"

Torren finishes my sentence. "—take over this world."

"We must stop her," Hansel demands.

I command the final gummy bear to do my bidding. The smell of green apples and mown grass overtakes the previous scents. "First, we track down Gretel."

Marlena's fingers trace the outline of the repaired charm. It sputters a weak caw but doesn't die. She nods. "If Veramis is messing with that kind of magic, we're in deeper trouble than we thought. The Witching Well isn't just some tourist attraction—it's a nexus of pure magical energy."

Izzy shakes her head in disbelief. "She wouldn't do that, would she?"

It's hard for her to accept her mother's duplicity. Not surprising. "She wants to be queen," I say. "Not only of the Dark Heart Court, but of everything."

"Including this world," Marlena adds.

"Why this world?" Izzy asks, perplexed. "No offense," she adds at Cyn's cough and Torren's raised brow.

"She has always wanted to be the high ruler of Ever After." The thought turns my stomach. "But she doesn't have the magic or enough soldiers to do it."

Torren catches the thread of my theory. "Becoming queen of Enchanted Haven gives her access to enslave the supernatural community, add to her magic reserves, and raise such an army."

I nod, a sour taste in my mouth that even the sweetest candy can't mask. "We have to stop her."

Hansel's jaw clenches. "We need to act fast. If Queen Veramis is already here, and she's done something to Gretel—"

The air in the shop turns charged, like right before a lightning strike. A strange prickling sensation crawls up my arms, and my attention is drawn to the tiny office off the workroom, where my mother's brooch rests. A muddy green light comes from it, spilling into the workroom. Cynric flinches. "What is that noise?"

I can't hear it, but the light intensifies. "I think we have a problem."

Magic crackles in the air, making the hairs on the back of my neck stand up. The very atmosphere in comes alive, humming with an otherworldly energy. I rush to the office, using a hand to shield my eyes. The brooch hovers above the desk and, at my nearness, shoots right at me.

Onyx responds, a barrier of my own magic blocking the dagger-like piece of jewelry.

It isn't detoured, though. It zips past me and into the workroom.

I scramble after it. A bolt of light shoots from the brooch, striking the repaired charm. Both artifacts rise into the air, spinning and twirling in an arcane dance.

"What in the name of sugar is happening?" I gasp, unable to tear my eyes away from the spectacle.

"It's like they're communicating." Izzy's voice quivers. "Fascinating, but also terrifying. Mostly terrifying."

The magical dance seems to set off a chain reaction throughout my beloved shop. Jars rattle on the shelves, the vibrant candies clinking against their glass confines. The jars lift into the air, orbiting around the spinning brooch and charm and nearly knocking all of us in our heads.

"Duck!" I yell as a display of heart-shaped lollipops whizzes past. "This is not good!"

Hansel yelps as jelly beans rain down around him. "Seraphina, do something!"

I take a deep breath, pushing down the panic in my chest. This is my shop, my magic. I can handle this. "Stay calm," I say, my voice steadier than I feel. "Marlena, contain the artifacts. Izzy, Hansel, grab the jars. And watch out for the—"

A loud crash interrupts as my brand new, prized chocolate fountain topples over. Even though it wasn't turned on, the cocoa chips have melted, and rivers of molten chocolate run across the floor. "—fountain," I finish with a sigh.

"It's like being inside a snow globe," Cyn says, snatching lollipops from the air.

Marlena raises her hands, and the air around us thickens with her magic. "Stand back," she warns, "unless you fancy being encased in sugar."

With a flourish of her hands, silvery threads dance around the brooch and charm, creating a shimmering cocoon. The clash of energies is almost visible, hers pulling inward while the artifacts force theirs out.

"Come now," Marlena murmurs as if coaxing a reluctant child. "That's enough mischief for one day."

Gradually, the chaos subsides. The air loses its electric charge, settling into a more familiar sweetness. We return the jars and lollipops to their shelves.

As the last of the disruption fades, we exchange glances. Hansel's hair is sticking up like he's been struck by lightning, and Izzy is covered in a fine dusting of powdered sugar. I'm sure I don't look much better.

"Well," I say, breaking the silence. "That was...something."

"Is everyone okay?" Torren asks, but his focus is on me.

Hansel nods, brushing some struck jelly beans from his shirt. "Takes more than that to take us down."

"Indeed," Marlena agrees. "Though I daresay we'll be finding candy in unexpected places for weeks to come."

As we clean up, I pick up the brooch and charm and examine them closely through the cocoon. The residual magic tingles against my fingertips, but Marlena has disconnected their odd link. "These two clearly have some serious mojo. Any theories as to why?"

"The energy signature is Queen Veramis's magic," my godmother states.

I shuffle through possibilities. "We suspect she gave the royal brooch to Cambria. Is it possible she stole it from Gretel, hexed it, and then gave it to the witch?"

"A strong possibility," Torren says.

Izzy brushes a finger over the crow. "But what about Gretel's charm? Did Mother do the same to it?"

"It's possible," Hansel chimes in, his voice grim. "If she's plotting to take over this world, these could be key components in her plan. I hope Gretel is all right."

I turn the charm over, thinking of Gretel and her cleverness. "What if Gretel purposely left this charm for us to find?"

Izzy's eyes widen. "Like a breadcrumb to lead us to her whereabouts."

"It's our best lead." I try to sound more confident than I feel. "I suspect she knows exactly what Veramis is up to, and yes, your Mother may have kidnapped Gretel or worse." I hate the emotions that cross Hansel and Izzy's faces at that statement, but we must face reality. "We need to figure out how these two are connected and, at the same time, find Gretel."

"It's late, and you've had a long day," Torren says. "You all need rest."

He's right, and although I want to argue and continue our quest, I see the haggard looks on Izzy and Hansel's faces. Marlena's, too. "We'll regroup in the morning. Come with your best ideas."

After they leave, I toss and turn in bed, unable to calm my thoughts. Cold sweeps through the room, and a familiar ghostly figure appears.

"Seraphina," our resident ghost boy whispers, his eyes wide with worry. "What happened in the shop... It's only the beginning. The magic has disturbed Enchanted Haven's balance. Dark times are coming."

I sit up, my heart pounding. "What do you mean?"

But he's already fading, leaving me alone with my fears and the looming mystery that threatens to engulf us all.

Chapter Six

Mayor Jo rushes in the following morning, bringing a gust of crisp morning air. His cheeks are flushed, either from the cold or something else entirely, as he beams at Marlena.

"Good morning," he says. "You're looking lovely as ever."

I stifle a giggle as Marlena rolls her eyes good-naturedly. The mayor's crush is about as subtle as a giant's footsteps.

"Coffee?" Marlena offers, gesturing to our freshly brewed pot. "And one of Seraphina's turnovers? They're still warm from the oven."

But Mayor Jo shakes his head, his expression turning serious. "I'm afraid I'll have to pass. We've got a situation at Faerie Bloom Garden Center, Sera. The plants have gone completely haywire—vines crawling up walls, flowers blooming out of season. It's utter chaos!"

My heart skips a beat. Is this what the ghost boy warned me about last night? I'd hoped it was just a sugar-induced dream, but apparently, it's not.

"Coming," I say, reaching for my coat. The aroma of cinnamon and caramelized apples fills the air, making my mouth water. I haven't eaten yet. "Let me grab a few things, and I'll head right over."

My godmother frowns. "The shop opens in an hour, and the whole group will be here to discuss our...you-know-what plans."

Mayor Jo eyes us suspiciously. "You-know-what plans?"

"For Valentine's Day," I say quickly. "It's a secret." At his grin, I realize he thinks it's about him and Marlena. Oops.

I draw her to the back and glance at the half-finished heart-shaped lollipops hardening on the worktable. They'll have to wait. "This is more important," I insist. "You handle the group. Listen to their ideas and make a plan. I'll be back as fast as I can."

Marlena sighs. "This is so like you," she murmurs. "Always ready to save the day, even if it means sacrificing your own ambitions."

A sleepy-eyed Hansel stumbles in, his hair tousled and eyes blinking against the early morning light. He slept in Izzy's room on the floor. "What's all the commotion?" He stifles a yawn.

I inform him about the garden center crisis as I don my coat, watching as his demeanor shifts from groggy to alert in seconds. His eyes sharpen with focus, and I can practically see the gears turning in his head. "Veramis," he mutters, reaching for his crossbow. "Sounds like we've got ourselves a magical mess to clean up."

As Hansel straps Dradus to his back, I pray he's wrong. "Always ready for battle, aren't you?" I tease, tossing him a coffee-flavored candy. "Have some sugar. You might need the energy."

He catches it deftly, popping it into his mouth before patting his weapon. "Better safe than sorry. You never know when the evil queen might decide to crash the party."

I grab a handful of cherry candies, stuffing them into my pockets alongside some licorice whips. "Let's hope she has nothing to do with this," I say, heading for the door. "Come on, we've got some plants to tame."

We rush into the brisk morning air, leaving the mayor to help Marlena prep the shop for customers. The sun pushes its way over the tops of buildings, scattering the shadows. Our breath forms clouds as we hurry down the streets. The usual sweet scents of Enchanted Haven are overshadowed by an undercurrent of something wild. It's earthy and green, with a layer of villainous energy that makes my skin tingle.

"Can you feel that?" I ask, my heart racing.

He nods, his face grim. "It's like the air itself is charged. Whatever's happening at Faerie Bloom, it's big."

As we approach the garden center, I'm hit by a wave of chaos. Mr. Thornwick, the usually composed owner, is practically dancing a jig of panic on the sidewalk, his hands flailing like he's trying to swat away invisible bees. "Oh, thank goodness you're here!" he cries, his eyes saucer-shaped. "It's a disaster, Ms. Fairchild! Utter botanical bedlam! The mayor said you could help me."

I lay a hand on his arm. "Deep breaths, Mr. Thornwick. Can you tell me exactly what happened?"

His mustache quivers. "It started last night. I heard strange noises, like giggling flowers." He shakes his head. "Insane, I know. When I came in this morning... Well, see for yourself!"

I turn to face the garden center, and my jaw drops. It's as if Mother Nature decided to throw a raucous party. Vines twist and curl up the walls like mischievous snakes, flowers bloom and un-bloom in a dizzying kaleidoscope of colors. I swear I can hear the plants groaning.

"This is not your average case of overzealous fertilizer," Hansel says, unslinging his crossbow. "Any ideas?"

I bite my lip, considering. "We need to get in there and take a closer look."

As we cross through the entrance, a tendril of ivy reaches out, almost playfully tugging at my sleeve. I bat it away.

Hansel fingers his weapon. "Let's show these overgrown weeds who's boss."

I pull out a handful of licorice strings, their sweet scent mingling with the heady aroma of herbs and flowers gone wild. "Time to put these babies to work."

I weave the licorice through the air, methodically creating an intricate web of restraints. As I work, the licorice strings wrap around vines, constricting their movement. They envelop flowers, gently coaxing them to close their petals. It's like conducting a bizarre botanical orchestra, and I'm the candy-powered maestro. The plants' leaves rustle in what I can only describe as indignation. "We're just going to calm things down a bit," I assure them.

Hansel lowers his crossbow. "Princess, you never cease to amaze me."

If only I could find his sister. "Don't let down your guard yet."

As the last of the plants settle, wrapped snugly in licorice cocoons, Mr. Thornwick joins us. The poor man looks like he's aged a decade in the last hour, his usually immaculate suit rumpled and smeared with dirt. "Oh, my babies. Will they be alright?"

"They should be." I hand him a cherry candy. "Was there

anything unusual that happened before your garden decided to throw this impromptu rave?"

He runs a shaky hand through his thinning hair, chomping on the candy with gusto. "There was a woman," he whispers, his eyes darting around as if she might suddenly appear. "She came in just before closing. I've never seen anyone like her before."

Everything inside me stills. "What did she look like?"

Mr. Thornwick squints at a nearby bush. "Tall, imposing. Hair as dark as a raven's wing with streaks of silver. And her eyes... They were silver. Silver and cold as ice."

Hansel squeezes the handle of his crossbow. "I knew this was her work."

"She asked about my more...exotic specimens," Mr. Thornwick continues. "Specifically, those with poisonous properties. I should have known better, but she was so persuasive. I showed her my rarest plants, including a cutting from the Mourning Willow."

Not good. "But that's—"

He cringes. "Toxic, yes. She seemed particularly interested in it. And now...well, this happened." He lowers his voice. "Thank you for using your skills."

He's not a supernatural, but he's one of the humans in town who knows of our existence. "Of course," I say, patting his arm. "But I fear an evildoer has visited you. You must not have any more dealings with her, okay?"

His gaze drops to the ground. "I understand. It's early in the season, but some folks are eager to get to gardening. How long will I need to keep those *restraints* on the plants?"

The garden center falls silent, save for the muffled rustling of the plants in question. "Twenty-four hours, at the very least.

Possibly longer." At his disappointed look, I reach for reassurance. "I'll do my best to nip the source of this unfortunate incident in the bud as soon as possible, but it may take a few days."

He stares at the plants with sadness. "I had another unusual visitor yesterday. She was lovely and spoke to the plants as if they understood her." He smiles at the recollection. "I believe some of them did."

Hansel and I exchange a hope-filled look. "Did she wear a red cloak?" he asks. He holds his hand at chest level. "About so tall? Brown hair?"

Mr. Thornwick scratches his chin as he nods. "She asked about the other visitor—the evil one. Wanted to know what she was interested in, what she'd touched. But honestly, she seemed more concerned about the plants' well-being than anything else."

Gretel had been here. But why would she be investigating Queen Veramis in secret? Why didn't she come to me?

Because, like Hansel, she still believes I killed Izzy. I'm an Outcast. It would be treason.

"Can you tell us anything else about her?" I fiddle with a cherry candy, the urge to eat it strong. "Did she say where she was headed next? If she was staying here in Enchanted Haven? Why was she looking for the woman after the toxic plants?"

He shakes his head. "No, I'm sorry. She left without so much as a goodbye."

Hansel straps his crossbow to his back. "May I look around?" He rolls up his sleeves, revealing the runes marking his skin. His air magic calls to the birds, who gather on the fences and trees, but he has a fair amount of earth magic himself. Along with the birds, many of the plants gravitate toward him. "I have a bit of a green thumb."

The rustling stops as he moves along the rows of contained bushes and plants. The shrubs, trees, and flora settle. My candy restraints, no longer necessary, dissolve on their own.

"Amazing," I murmur. I've forgotten his connection to nature is as strong and steady as his loyalty to his friends and family.

By the time Hansel returns to us, Mr. Thornwick is grinning. Hansel looks a bit tired but satisfied. "There," he says with a small smile. "That should do it."

Mr. Thornwick shakes his hand enthusiastically. "I can't thank you enough."

Just as I relax at the fact that the garden center is back to normal, a shimmering mist materializes in the central area. It swirls and coalesces into the form of Flower, the town's resident ghost, wearing what appears to be a Victorian-era ball gown made entirely of cotton candy.

"There you are!" she chirps, her translucent form bobbing gently in the air. "I heard there was a commotion over here. Thought I'd see what all the fuss is about."

"You know, Hansel, perhaps you could help Mr. Thornwick right those toppled fruit trees in the back corner," I say, aware that only I can see and hear her.

They walk off, chatting about flowers, birds, and gardening.

Flower twirls in her gossamer gown, sending sparkles of spirit energy through the air. "My, my, what lovely plants," she says, drifting toward pots of tulips and crocus. "I do hope the butterflies are enjoying this unexpected feast."

"It's February. There aren't any butterflies yet."

She appears utterly confused. "Time is such a fickle thing when you're eternal. I really wish there were butterflies."

"Not today," I say, "but I could use your help. My friend Gretel is missing. She visited here yesterday and was in Whimsy Park, wearing a red cloak. Have you, by chance, noticed her anywhere?"

Her perpetually innocent expression is replaced by an uncharacteristic seriousness. Her ethereal form seems to flicker. "Seraphina, dear," she says, her voice dropping to a whisper, "there's a book at Spellbound Books you simply must see."

My ears perk up, but my heart sinks. Flower is forever distracted by the most innocuous things. Like butterflies. "I don't need a book. I need to locate Gretel."

Her eyes dart about as if checking for eavesdroppers. "It's an ancient tome surrounded by a bubble of ugly energy. The pages speak of a magic that can twist time. But time is of the essence. Get it?" Her serious face morphs back into her normal expression. "Hurry, Sera!"

I glance at my watch, and my heart sinks. It's almost opening time at the shop. I call to Hansel. "We need to get to the bookshop. It may be a dead end, but it may be another clue."

As Hansel and I say our goodbyes to Mr. Thornwick, I wonder if this is a wild goose chase. The early morning dew on the lawns has disappeared, and the town is just beginning to stir.

"What do you think we'll find in this book?" Hansel asks.

"Maybe nothing. Flower is unreliable at best."

We round the corner, and the bookstore comes into view. Its quaint facade, with a slightly crooked sign and window boxes overflowing with enchanted flowers that never die, always reminds me of the gingerbread houses from my childhood. Only less likely to fatten you up for a witch's dinner.

The owner is just opening up as we arrive. As we enter, a phone rings in the background, and she greets us even as she rushes off to answer it. The familiar scent of old parchment, leather, and ink envelops us as we scan the shelves, ready to uncover whatever clue might await.

Chapter Seven

The place reminds me of countless hours poring over magical books in Ever After. Most often, Izzy was beside me. Sometimes Gretel, and even Hansel, were, too.

The floorboards creak beneath our feet. "Where should we start?"

"Your guess is as good as mine." Hansel waves a hand. "Lead the way, Princess."

We make our way through the maze-like aisles, squeezing past towering shelves that seem to lean in curiously as we pass.

"By the kingdom," Hansel mutters, ducking under a low-hanging chandelier. "This place is like the Black Forest, but with books instead of evil trees."

I chuckle softly. "And hopefully, no Big Bad Wolf waiting to gobble us up."

Onyx and my internal magic alarm both alert me to an unusual fluctuation in the air as we near the rear of the store. That's when I see it. Nestled between two towering stacks of grimoires, a dusty silver tome calls to me. Its ornate cover emits a cold energy. My heart races as I reach out, my fingertips brushing against the worn leather.

It doesn't zap me, and Onyx remains on alert but doesn't heat. "This is it," I breathe, carefully pulling it from its resting place.

Hansel steps back. "Be careful. We don't know what kind of magic might be bound to the pages."

I appreciate his concern, but my excitement gives me an energy boost. Opening the cover, the musty scent of ancient paper wafts out, and my fingers nearly tremble as I spy the intricate illustrations sprawling across the yellowed pages. "Oh, Hansel," I whisper. "I think we've just opened a whole new chapter in our faerytale."

I run my finger gently along the delicate script, tracing familiar names woven into the tale. Hansel peers over my shoulder, his warm presence a comfort as we delve deeper into the book's secrets.

"Veramis," I murmur, my voice barely audible in the hushed atmosphere of the shop. "It's all here, her rise to power, her ambitions. It's our story, but a very different version."

"In this one, she seeks to control not only the Black Heart Court but both realms." He rears back. "Just like you and the nightwalker speculated."

I read farther ahead, not liking how the story turns out. My stomach twists in knots, and I feel lightheaded. There is no happy ending for any of us. "How can we stop someone so powerful? What if we're already too late?"

"We've faced many challenges before," Hansel says softly, placing a reassuring hand on my shoulder. "We'll figure this one out."

I'm grateful for his unwavering certainty. I feel none of it, however. I fake my confidence. "We simply need to approach this like an intricate recipe. Break it down, gather our ingredients, and create something unexpected."

Hansel grins, some of the tension easing from his shoulders. He's not as confident as he wants me to believe, but now that I'm on board, he grows more so. "What's our first step, oh master confectioner?"

The shop's doorbell chimes. I glance toward the front, and my breath catches. Torren's presence is as commanding as ever. My blood heats as our eyes lock.

A curious smile plays at the corners of his mouth as he approaches, his gaze flicking to the book in my hands. "What have you two uncovered?"

I feel a flutter in my stomach—that mix of attraction and unease that always accompanies his appearance. I straighten my spine, determined to focus on the task at hand. "Something terribly concerning."

His eyebrow arches elegantly. "I assumed so from the look on your face. Tell me."

"It's about Veramis. This is a faerytale that details her rise to power and her rivalry with my mother." As I speak, I can taste the bitterness of the tale on my tongue. "She's not content with ruling the Black Heart Court. Veramis wants control over both realms—Ever After and this one. Perhaps even more."

Torren's eyes narrow, a flicker of concern passing over his features. He takes the book from me and flips through the pages, reading at an incredible speed before he snaps it shut. "As we suspected," he murmurs. "Things are more serious than a simple kidnapping."

"We have to protect both worlds," I declare, my voice carrying determination and barely concealed fear. "Veramis is a threat to all we hold dear."

"But there's more, isn't there?" he asks. "Something you were about to share last night before we were interrupted."

The shop suddenly feels more diminutive, the towering bookshelves closing in around me. "You're right," I admit, my voice barely above a whisper. "There is something else."

Hansel replaces the book on the shelf and takes my hand. "What is it, Princess?"

The memory tickles over my skin, raising the hair on the back of my neck. "I felt someone watching me yesterday. Like a shadow I couldn't shake." The words tumble out, sticky and edged with vinegar. "At first, I thought I was being paranoid, but now I think it was Veramis. I *know* it was."

Hansel squeezes my hand. "I won't let any harm come to you," he declares, his voice as steady as a mountain.

The rush of affection for my friend warms me like hot cocoa on a chilly day. Not to be outdone, Torren moves forward, his tall frame filling the aisle. "While I appreciate your enthusiasm, Hansel,"—his voice is smooth as caramel—"I believe I'm better equipped to ensure Seraphina's safety. After all, I do have centuries of experience in these matters."

The tension between them is suddenly as thick as nougat. I can practically see the sparks flying as they lock eyes, each trying to outdo the other in their promises of protection.

"With all due respect, Master Vampyre," Hansel retorts, his hand moving to Dradus. "I am in the Royal Guard. I've been trained since childhood to guard against threats like Veramis. This is literally what I was born to do."

Males and their egos. It's like watching two knights squabble over who gets to slay the dragon.

"Gentlemen," I interject, trying to keep my voice light despite the worry gnawing at my insides, "I'm hardly a damsel in distress. Perhaps we could focus on the actual threat?"

Hansel's cheeks flush slightly, and even Torren looks a bit sheepish. It's almost enough to make me forget the constant prickle of unease at the back of my neck, the feeling that somewhere, somehow, Veramis is watching...waiting...planning her next move in this twisted faerytale we've found ourselves in.

"Of course," Torren says. "Our priority should be unraveling this mystery and protecting both realms."

"And rescuing Gretel," Hansel adds.

If I know my friend, she would take umbrage at that statement. Like me, she does not consider herself ever in need of rescuing. Still, without knowing what's happened to her, we must consider all possible circumstances. "I think our next step is clear."

"It is?" Hansel asks.

I grab the magic book and tuck it under my arm. "We need to get back to The Candy Cauldron. It's our base of operations, and we have a big dragon to slay."

The owner emerges from the back, and I pay for the book.

We step into the street, and I inhale sharply as the cool air hits my face. It's a stark contrast to the warm, dusty interior of the bookshop, and it helps clear my head.

"First things first," I say, my mind already churning with ideas as we hustle back to the shop, "we need to decode the story in this book. There are clues here as to Veramis' next move."

"Cyn can work on that," Torren says. "He's good with chronicles and fables."

The Witching Well in the town square bubbles merrily. A group of young women passes by, their laughter reminding me of tinkling bells.

"What about me?" Hansel prompts. "Where should I look next for Gretel if the charm can't locate her?"

I square my shoulders. "You and Torren need to plan our defense. If Veramis is watching my every move, we must be ten steps ahead of her."

"Always thinking ahead," the vampyre says with a hint of pride in his voice. "Your cunning is one of the reasons I enjoy working with you."

I elbow him in the ribs. "Less flirting, more focus. We've got realms to save." *And I have the Valentine's festival to bake for.*

As we near my candy shop, its whimsical storefront coming into view, I feel a renewed sense of purpose. I push open the door to the sweet aroma of sugar and spices, already feeling better. This is my sanctuary, my realm of magic.

Customers are in line at the counter, Marlena and Izzy working fast as they wait on them. They both give me questioning glances, but we can't discuss what's happened with a packed crowd. I gesture the men to the back to get started on their assignments while I pull on an apron to help customers.

Marlena removes a twig from my hair. "Everything go okay with the plants?"

"Back to normal, and I have plenty to tell you at break time."

As I work, I feel Torren's watchful gaze on me. When I take an empty tray to the back to refill it, his voice is soft as he comes up behind me. "You truly are remarkable, you know. A force to be reckoned with."

I feel a blush creeping up my cheeks, but I keep my eyes on my task to prevent him from seeing it. "Save the sweet talk for later when this is all over."

He leans into my hair, and I feel his lips curve into a smile. "It will be my pleasure, Princess."

Chapter Eight

The back room hums with the intensity of a beehive. Sticky pieces of candy cling to my apron and hair, and trays of assorted cookies and candies line every surface. I almost feel ready for the festival.

At the worktable, Marlena rolls out fondant with the precision of a general commanding dough troops. Her too-tight curls bounce with tension as she mutters about mortal buttercream being "tragically unmagical" under her breath.

Izzy's tongue pokes out between her teeth in concentration as she pipes icing onto heart-shaped shortbread. Or rather, *attempts* to pipe it. The fifth cookie in a row now sports a squiggle that looks less like "Be Mine" and more like "Bemused Ins."

"Be gentle," I instruct. I focus on swirling iridescent glitter into a batch of enchanted gumdrops and turn to Marlena. "Did you finish that chapter about Veramis? The part where she dueled with my mother and won?"

A sigh escapes her tight lips. "Power's a thirsty beast, Sera. It rarely stops at one sip."

"But that isn't the real story," Izzy says. "Queen Lethia is *the* Queen of Ever After. My mother is only head of the Black Heart Court, not the entire realm."

"There are many versions of each and every story," I remind her. Cynric has the alternate faerytale story. Torren and Hansel are at the church with him, developing defensive strategies based on what the book claims might happen. "This alternate version has found its way here, which makes it possible it has the power to come true."

A loud *pop* makes Marlena and I jump. Izzy's icing bag has exploded across the end of the table in a pink carnage.

"Sorry," she whispers.

I'm around the end before the first tear escapes her eye. "It's all right. Do you need to lie down?"

Her dark eyes swim with unfocused panic. "My memories keep tangling up. It's like when you drop a music box and all the gears spill out." She presses trembling fingers covered in frosting to her temple. "Every time I start to remember that night—the night we fought, and I died—everything shifts. Even your face blurs in the memory now, and I—"

She gasps, knees buckling. I catch her elbow as Marlena rushes to her other side, doing the same.

"Third migraine this week," Marlena observes. "All this going on with Veramis and Hansel coming back into the picture...her memories are forcing their way into the limelight, ready for them or not."

We guide Izzy to a chair at the break table. She makes a face, wiping frosting from her cheek. "I'm dying. I'm sure of it. The curse is too strong."

Marlena presses a chilled lavender sachet to her forehead. "Hush, child. Let the professionals argue over your impending doom."

But I see the worry lining Marlena's eyes as she mouths *memory suppression* over Izzy's bent head. The unspoken truth weighs heavy in my stomach—every time Izzy fights to recall the false murder that exiled me, the spell fights back.

Marlena points at the shelf of herbal concoctions. I nod. "Right. Tea should help." I gather what I need for a calming blend. "Chamomile, rosehips, a pinch of oblivion root—just enough to take the edge off, not enough to make you forget your own name."

"That happened *once*," Izzy mutters. "And isn't that counterintuitive to helping me remember the truth?"

I mentally catalog the tremor in her hands as she moves the sachet to the back of her neck. "We can skip the oblivion root. Perhaps it would be best to go with plain chamomile?"

Marlena rummages through clay jars labeled in her spidery cursive. "Dragon's Sneeze, Mermaid Tears, ah, here it is— Migraine Masala. Perfect. Let's try this."

The clatter of porcelain jars fills the kitchen as I pull out our chipped blue teapot, shaped like a grinning toad with steam puffing through its nostrils. Izzy slumps over the table, closing her eyes.

"It's getting worse," I whisper to my godmother, handing her my mix of herbs to add to her migraine potion. "Last week, she forgot to add the sugar to the sugar cookies. Yesterday, I heard her call Gunther 'that chatty butter knife.'"

Marlena tosses the herbs into the toad's gaping mouth. "Memory spells are like termites. You don't notice the damage until the whole roof caves in."

"Comforting."

As the tea brews, steam coils into shapes—a rose, a crown, a dagger. The meaning of the crown and dagger seem obvious

—Queen Veramis stabbing me and everyone else in the back. The rose less so.

Izzy lifts her head and points at the sugar bowl. "Remember when we tried to make that truth-telling taffy? Burned off half your eyebrows?"

After adding a spoonful of sugar to the blend, I pour the golden liquid into a mug. "You told me I rocked the 'singed crown princess vibe.'"

Her laugh turns into a wince halfway through. She sips the brew, then clutches her temple, sloshing tea onto the saucer. "Still tastes like defeat. Needs more..."

"Sugar?" I push the bowl toward her.

"Fireball whisky," Marlena says, pouring a cup of tea for herself.

I join in, the tea calming my nerves.

Izzy consumes three mugs worth. Her leg starts jiggling under the table, rattling our cups. "This is useless." She slams down her mug. "I can still feel it—like a swarm of beetles trapped behind my eyes trying to drill their way out with tiny jackhammers."

Marlena catches my gaze over Izzy's head. A silent conversation unfolds in raised eyebrows and tightened lips. *Alchemy Elixirs?* her look suggests.

Last resort, I reply. The shop is a curiosity and a resource. The owner, however, is not my favorite.

She's deteriorating, Marlena counters.

Lady Wyndolynn waltzes through, turning her pert nose up at the frosting that landed on the floor. The cat purrs, and in my head, I hear, *Your godmother speaks the truth. You should listen.*

I fill her bowl with her favorite salmon kibble as Mr. Nibbles drags up his courage and races from his home inside the kitchen wall to gather crumbs into his cheeks. He looks more like a ground squirrel than a mouse before he races back to his hiding place right before Wynnie slams down a paw behind him.

"Fine." I swipe a dish towel embroidered with dancing whisks. "But if Ms. Nyssa tries to sell us another 'youth serum' made of snail mucus..."

"That's disgusting." Izzy stands too fast, swaying into the cooling racks. "Do the humans know she's doing that?"

"You should stay here," I tell her. "We'll see what she has for migraines. And no, they have no idea that she's using magic spells, not unique ingredients, to cause their wrinkles to disappear."

"False advertising," Marlena says.

Izzy rights herself and slips her coat on. "I'm going with you."

Marlena grabs Gunther and hangs him on her belt, covering him with her coat.

"Do you think we'll need that?" Izzy asks.

"With Vermis watching?" Marlena says. "We can't be too careful."

The festival banners slap against lampposts as we make our way to Alchemy Elixirs & Remedies. A lavender-colored evening is upon us, but plenty of folks are out, the coming festival lifting their winter doldrums.

Izzy pauses to squint at a window display of valentines. "'Roses are red, violets are blue, if you break my heart, I'll turn you into—'"

I hook her elbow, steering her on. "Focus. Migraine first, poetic threats later."

The shop is on a side street, wedged between an accounting firm and a barbershop. Alchemy Elixirs & Remedies doesn't so much have a door as a portal—a writhing curtain of beads that hisses as we push through, signaling the owner that we're supernaturals.

"Lovely," Izzy coughs, batting away incense smoke. "Smells like a dragon's gym bag in here."

Shelves curve inward like a carnivorous plant's gullet, glass vials pulsing with bioluminescent glows. Something croons from the shadowy rafters. Ms. Nyssa materializes behind the counter, her braided hair threaded with what I dearly hope aren't finger bones.

"The candy witch. You brought your entourage." Her smile reveals teeth filed to delicate points. "Here for more of my youth potion? You are looking a bit haggard, Sera. Or perhaps..." Her gaze lands on Izzy's twitching left eye. "Something for your ailing friend?"

"She's having migraines," I tell the woman, skipping the details. "We need something to relieve the pain."

Her clawed fingers drum the countertop. "Let me guess— headaches localized behind the left temple? Sudden vertigo when attempting to recall specific events? Can't stop humming annoying show tunes?"

"I do not," Izzy insists.

"Actually, you've been stuck on *Be Our Guest* for days," Marlena counters.

"Beauty and the Beast is my favorite," Izzy mutters. "It gives me hope."

I pat her arm. "We've tried a variety of potions and herbs. None have helped."

Izzy ambles along the glass display, rubbing her temples as

she examines the contents. "I have a beetle convention in my sinuses."

Ms. Nyssa plucks a vial of swirling indigo liquid from a shelf, puts it back. "Symptoms suggest suppressed memories fighting to surface. Like champagne bubbles trapped under duct tape." She leans across the counter, bone beads clacking. "Who cast the spell?"

The question hangs between us, sharp as her filed teeth. Should have known she'd put two and two together. "That doesn't matter," I say. "We just need a pain reliever."

"I can't treat frostbite with mittens, Miss Fairchild. Not unless I know whether the ice came from between a penguin's toes or from a jilted Eskimo's tears."

Behind me, Marlena murmurs, "It's always the jilted ones."

"So, you have nothing to ease her symptoms?" I challenge. "Guess we'll be on our way."

Ms. Nyssa's sigh makes the candle flames gutter. She rummages under the counter, bottles clinking before she brings out a cobalt blue jar. "Two drops under the tongue. Side effects may include spontaneous haiku, temporary invisibility, or an irresistible urge to knit sweaters for stray cats."

Izzy uncaps it and shows me the murky green potion inside. "What's the base ingredient? Please say it's not another snail mucus potion."

"Memory moss harvested from tombstones." Ms. Nyssa portions the sludge into a thimble-sized cup. "Stirred counter-clockwise during a waning moon by a bard with perfect pitch. Or was it a barber? Details get fuzzy after the seventh whiskey."

As she speaks, a dried caterpillar slips from her sleeve. She flicks it away. "Not as potent as what Gretel can brew, but serviceable."

I freeze, as do the others. "Gretel? You know her?"

Ms. Nyssa also freezes. Above us, the creeping vines framing the shelves shiver, curling inward like protective spines. "Small towns breed tall tales. One hears whispers of forest guardians, cursed royals..." Her smile stretches too wide as she pins me with frank appraisal. "Foolish children nibbling on enchanted real estate."

Marlena edges toward the counter, her hand on Gunther's hilt. "Do you often dispense remedies to foolish children?"

"Only those who pay upfront." The shopkeeper slides the cup toward Izzy. "Thirty dollars. Or that recipe for crystallized gingersnaps you refuse to share."

Izzy downs the sludge and then makes a disgusted sound. "Tastes like diseased rosemary and dirt. Gross."

I hand over the money—I don't share recipes—and press a handkerchief to Izzy's chin, where green droplets escaped. "Better?"

She blinks, pupils dilating. "The wall sconces... Why are they breathing?"

Ms. Nyssa pockets the payment. "Side effects fade within the hour. Unlike memories." Her pointed look lingers on Izzy, now tracing finger patterns in the dust motes. "Certain things stay buried for good reason."

Marlena herds us toward the exit. "Time to go, ladies."

Onyx hasn't heated, and I need to ask more questions. I brush away my godmother's hand. "Was Gretel here? In a red cloak?"

"Who?" Ms. Nyssa asks, all innocence.

Marlena is demanding as she grasps my arm and hauls me to the door. I pause at the threshold, sunlight slicing through the grimy window. "If she returns, please call us."

Ms. Nyssa's reflection fragments in the hanging prism above her. "Why would she?"

Those who meddle with queens and curses...

I blink, frowning at her. "What was that?"

Her shrug sets the bone charms chattering. "The woman you seek has no reason to come here."

...either become legends or cautionary fables.

Izzy stumbles out onto the sidewalk. Marlena jerks me out alongside her. "She was trying to place a spell on you," my godmother scolds.

"Onyx didn't react."

My argument gets me nowhere. "The gargoyle was entranced, too."

"That's never happened before."

Marlena sends the three of us marching toward Main Street. "Because Nyssa isn't playing with her normal magical potions anymore. She's upped her game. Queen-level magic."

"At least my headache's gone," Izzy says.

But apparently, Veramis has a new partner in crime. "We destroyed the connection between Veramis and Cambria, so the queen has found a new witch to work with."

Once inside The Candy Cauldron, the shop wraps around us, whisking away the scent of bitter herbs from Alchemy Elixirs with vanilla bean and dark cocoa. I press my palms against the worn worktable, welcoming its familiar feel.

Home.

The phone rings. A customer wants three pounds of mint fudge for Valentine's Day cut into bite-size chunks for a party. I close my eyes, forcing a smile as I assure her I'll have her order ready by tomorrow afternoon. The moment we say our good-byes, I start grabbing ingredients.

"Don't you think I should try connecting to Gretel?" Izzy asks.

"Not until Torren and Hansel have a plan for any potential

outcomes that might bring," I say. "Besides, between the poisoning and the migraine, you need rest. When you try to connect with her, it could be a magical force that needs all of your strength to work."

"Right," she says, disappointed.

"We've got orders to fill." I hand several to Marlena and take the others for myself. "And I want to talk to Flower again before we tangle with Veramis next."

"The ghost?" Izzy plucks a lemon twist from the 'imperfections' bowl, nibbling it. Her pupils still hold that tea-saucer wideness from Ms. Nyssa's potion. "Why?"

"She might have more insights."

Marlena and I fall into an old rhythm, and Izzy refuses to go to bed.

"It's still there, isn't it?" I ask her at one point when she stops piping frosting and stares at the floor. "The fog."

Marlena's ladle pauses mid-pour. "Mists often lift once you stop glaring at them."

Izzy snaps back to blink at us. "Easy for you to say. You're not the one with half your memories pickled."

The front bell chimes—not our shop's friendly tinkle, but the harsh clang of someone shoving the door open. "Didn't you lock up?" Marlena asks.

"I did," I say.

We discover the fortune teller, Madam Zara, standing at the display case, her turban askew and scarves fluttering. "I found your ghost."

I glance around. "Sorry, what?"

Her bangles clink as she hitches a thumb over her shoulder. "She was hovering around my tent near the Witching Well, crying. Said she needed the candy shop witch. That's you, right?"

Smoky tendrils appear behind her. As I peer closer, I see Flower's face slightly obscured by them. She stares at me from her round glasses with a look of distress. "Help me," she whimpers.

"Oh dear," Izzy says. Being from the Dark Heart Court, she can see spirits. At least, she used to.

"You can see her?" I ask. "Is your gift back?"

Izzy nods but doesn't seem happy about it. "This is the one you told us about?"

"Yes, Flower." I motion for the ghost to come out from behind Madam Zara. "It's okay, now. You're safe. What happened?"

"She's alive!" The fortune teller gasps, slamming both palms on the display case. The racks inside rattle. But it isn't her voice—it's Flower's. "In the woods! Under a sleeping spell! The crows won't stop crying!"

The back door opens and closes. Hansel runs in. "What is she talking about?"

"Who?" I ask Flower. My voice comes out quieter than I intend. "Gretel?"

Madame Zara's kohl-rimmed eyes roll back. "The ghouls walk between worlds, but the faery bridge is crumbling! Three days! Three days before the queen's shadow swallows—"

A chocolate heart explodes in the display window. Madam Zara slumps to the floor. Flower hovers above her, her hair singed and the smoky tendrils weaving around her on a phantom breeze. "I don't feel so good, Sera," she says, and she faints, too.

Chapter Nine

Hansel carries Madam Zara to the back room. "What just happened?"

"Make more tea," I tell Marlena. "Something strong and black. We're going to need it."

"Trouble?" I jump at Torren's velvet-smooth voice. The vampyre lord fills the back doorway like spilled ink given human form. His charcoal suit blends with the twilight beyond. Cynric peers over his shoulder.

"Too much of it," I say.

They enter, and Cynric helps himself to a cookie. "You've got goo in your hair." His eyes flick upward.

We revive the fortune teller and bring the three men up-to-date on what we suspect concerning Ms. Nyssa.

Flower also regains consciousness and levitates in the corner. "She attacked me." She searches out my gaze. "Why did she attack me?"

"Who attacked you? What did she look like?"

"Tall, silvery eyes, cold. She was so cold."

"Veramis," Hansel says.

Marlena speaks a spell, and suddenly, all the others can see Flower, not just me and Izzy. "That was you talking through Madame Zara. You said she's alive—did you mean Gretel?"

Flower nods slowly, her attention catching on the slithering smoke around her. "I heard her crying, and I tried to talk to her. I thought it was the tree, but then I realized it might be that person you're looking for. That's when that awful woman attacked me."

"Mother," Izzy says, her voice filled with disappointment. After everything we've learned about Veramis, it says something that she still can feel emotion over this latest action. Even with everything she knows about her mother, she must still have been holding out hope that Veramis has a good reason for what she's doing.

"I don't know how to heal a ghost," I tell my godmother. "Do you?"

Izzy moves toward Flower. "I'm sorry this happened to you." She turns to me. "We need to boil moss, grind up some toadstools, and add grave dirt. We'll also need a mirror."

"I'll get the moss and toadstools," Marlena says.

Torren grabs Cyn. "We'll get the graveyard dirt."

"How much do you need?" Cyn asks, snagging a second cookie.

Izzy digs through my stash of pots until she finds a copper one. "Ten ounces should do."

While they gather ingredients, I send Hansel to take the mirror in my bedroom from the wall. Madam Zara pulls out tarot cards and shuffles. "Seems like someone is in dire trouble, and I don't mean the ghost."

Hansel returns, handing the mirror to me and peering at

the cards she's placed on the break table. "Spit it out, fortuneteller," he growls. "If my sister's knee-deep in trouble—"

"Your sister's knee-deep in fir needles," Madame Zara snaps. The overhead light catches her milky eyes as she slaps down the Tower card. "There are shadows in the woods with too many teeth circling her."

Hansel nearly yanks her from the chair. "Which woods?"

Marlena returns from the backyard where our small garden resides. Although it is still mostly dormant, she has managed to find moss and a few spindly mushrooms.

"The trees have black bark," Madam Zara says. "They smell of rotting flowers and charred earth. Like a cemetery florist's dumpster."

"The Black Forest." I glance at Marlena for her confirmation. She nods. "But that only exists in Ever After."

Marlena shakes her head. "Veramis can create a version of it anywhere if she has enough trees. We know Gretel was here, and your ghost friend heard her in a tree."

"Is she hiding, or is she imprisoned?" Hansel demands.

Neither the fortuneteller nor Flower responds. Flower shrugs and stares at the shadowy smoke still twining about her form.

Torren and Cynric return, dropping a bag of dirt on the worktable. "Will this do?" Torren asks.

It's from the pet cemetery behind the church. "It will have to," Izzy says. She throws the ingredients into the copper pot, murmuring over them as they heat.

"Could Veramis be using Whimsy Park as her Black Forest?" I ask.

Marlena frowns. "If so, I should have sensed her magic there."

"As should I," Izzy says, stirring the pot. "I didn't."

"The vines attacked us, though." I watch the ropes of Veramis' magic encircling Flower. "This is all her, one hundred percent, no matter if you sensed her magic or not. I did. She was watching us, I'm sure of it."

"There are thirty-seven wooded areas within a hundred-mile radius of town," Cynric says, catching on. "If it's not Whimsy Park, we have a much bigger area to search."

"You'll need divination," Madam Zara insists, pulling out a pendulum.

"I don't need your tricks to find family." Hansel's throat bobs as he glares at the tarot cards. "Just a good pair of boots and my common sense."

Izzy removes the boiling concoction from the stove. "Flower, come here."

The ghost hesitates, and I nod when she glances at me. "You can do this," I tell her.

Izzy pours a thin layer of the hot liquid on the mirror, chunks of moss spilling out. "Look into the mirror, Flower. Imagine yourself floating on its surface."

Madam Zara comes to the table and peers into the mirror, too. "What does it do?"

Flower bats at her. "Hey, this is my ride. Get your own."

In the next instant, the ghost bends forward to stare into the reflective surface. The smoke trails stop floating around her, and she becomes immobile, her eyes widening. There's a slight pop, and the mirror sucks the tendrils into it.

"Grab her," Izzy yells, and Hansel and Torren both reach out.

But Flower is a ghost. I don't expect them to be able to hold on.

Yet, they do because the chunks of moss fly off the mirror's surface and stick to Flower right where their hands land.

The mirror shudders and makes a final slurping noise. All the liquid disappears, as does the last of the smoke. Flower staggers as a wave of fresh air flows through the room. Her hair returns to normal, and the fear in her eyes subsides. She giggles. "Wow, that was a trip."

Torren and Hansel release her. I press a palm over the Tower card's crumbling castle image. "Common sense says charging blindly into cursed forests gets you eaten. We need—"

"A tracker," Torren interrupts. "Someone familiar with Veramis' proclivities."

Izzy cleans up the mirror with Hansel's help. "Where's the charm, Sera?"

I've wrapped it and the brooch in separate leather bags. I retrieve it, and she takes it from me, unwrapping the material and opening the bag. She holds it up. "What if we use this like a pendulum over a map?"

"Not a bad idea," I say. "Cyn, can you provide maps of the woods?"

"We don't need maps or pendulums," Hansel says. "Hold the charm and find my sister, Isadora!"

She glances away. "I already tried. It didn't work." I arch a brow at her. She shrugs. "When you were gone. I wanted to be helpful, and I thought it might work."

Hansel marches for the door. "I will simply interrogate every tree from here to Ever After until I find her."

Torren blocks his path. "Trees rarely appreciate midnight interrogations."

"Move, bat."

"Children," Marlena barks. The overhead lights flicker

violet. "Arguing won't get us anywhere." She points at me. "We need to warn your parents of Veramis's intent."

She's right. I should have already done it. "I'll have Trinken take a message to them." The goblin will be none too happy to do my bidding, but he will.

Hansel rams his shoulder against Torren's arm. "Try stopping me again. See what happens."

Cynric rummages through the container of conversation hearts. "They'll be at this all night, won't they?"

Hansel vibrates with barely contained fury. "Assuming Gretel's within auditory range of sentient trees—which, given the migratory patterns of enchanted flora in this realm, seems statistically improbable—we require—"

"Your sister isn't a probability curve," Torren says.

Hansel grunts and continues as if uninterrupted. "At a minimum, we need directional markers. Perhaps Izzy can spell the crow charm and calibrate it."

"Or," Marlena interrupts, "we turn the tables on Veramis and let her lead us to Gretel."

"Dark armies require two things," Torren says. "Soldiers, and something to make them obey. We find Veramis' current army camp, dismantle her operations, and—"

"And rescue Gretel," I finish firmly.

Cynric nods, pulling out his phone. "If we cross-reference recent missing persons reports with areas of concentrated magical residue, that will tell us where the camp is."

"This army isn't human," Marlena tells him. "It's a shadow army. There won't be any missing persons. They obey Veramis because she's created them and programmed them to follow her commands."

"Tell us more," Torren says. "We need to know everything about our enemy."

As she and Hansel fill him and Cynric in, I slip into the backyard, the waning moon the only light. My fingers tremble as I shape a candy sparrow from a handful of caramels—extra wing reinforcement to survive the journey.

Torren joins me unexpectedly. His shadow stretches across the herb garden, making the rosemary bushes shiver. "Will your parents mobilize the Royal Guard?"

I press a message into the candy bird's belly. I don't have time to call the goblin and do things the old-fashioned way. "That's my hope. I must prepare them so they and the citizens of Ever After aren't ambushed."

The sparrow is about to take flight when a voice grumbles from the dormant jasmine archway. "Princess, really? Caramel couriers are so last century."

"Fair evening," I say.

Trinken steps into the moonlit garden like he's hitting a runway, his emerald-green suit clashing magnificently with his tan skin. "Message for your parents?"

I hand him the bird. "Your timing is impeccable. I'll owe you a favor."

The goblin inclines his head in acceptance—royal favors are rare, and he and I have already done a similar trade. "Your parents are mustering forces along the Shadow Peaks' border, you know. Your mother's been reinforcing the portal between here and Ever After."

My relief is palpable. "She suspects Veramis' plans?"

As a fellow Outcast, he has limited access to the realm but knows most of the happenings. "I know not why, only that there is unrest in the kingdom."

Behind us, the screen door bangs open. "Hansel and Izzy tried to spell the charm," Cynric announces, wiping what looks like raspberry jam from his eyebrow. "We require adult supervision."

Trinken inclines his head again, this time in goodbye. Torren and I return inside as Cynric leaves to fetch a map from his place.

Hansel paces the back room. Izzy gives me a meek, apologetic look at the donut-filling explosion all over the table, floor, and walls. We all pitch in to clean it up, and Cynric returns and spreads his map across the worktable. It's not a normal map—the forests keep rearranging themselves whenever he taps potential spots for Veramis' Black Forest version. "Why is the map doing that?" he asks.

Marlena fingers Gunther, now strapped to her waist. "Because of the spell Madam Zara mentioned—it's keeping the exact location unknown."

The fortuneteller is gone. I assume she had nothing left to offer, and Marlena sent her on her way.

Hansel surveys the map using a frosting knife rather than his finger to pinpoint locations. This seems to keep the landmarks still. "Gretel could be anywhere from here to these bluffs."

Izzy holds the charm over the map. "Let's see what this does."

Three things happen at once.

Everyone's cell phone bursts into a disco version of *I Wonder* from Sleeping Beauty.

The charm launches itself toward the front display window.

Every enchanted confection in a six-foot radius decides this is the perfect time to revolt.

"Incoming!" I duck as a swarm of champagne truffles fire almond slivers. Across the room, the sentient gingerbread house unfolds cookie limbs and makes a break for the back door.

Torren appears beside me in that unsettling vampyre way. "You're bleeding."

I wipe red goo from my cheek. "Nope. It's raspberry filling."

He sighs but stops a charging gummy bear mid-pounce using only a raised finger. Showoff.

Izzy perches atop the worktable. "It's the brooch! It's creating a feedback loop!"

My eyes dart to said brooch, lying on the break table. "What's that doing in here?" Snatching it up amid a series of flying gumballs, I clutch the royal pin to my chest. It pulses with my heartbeat.

"Put it in the copper pan," Izzy says. "It will break the connection."

I slam it into the pan. The resulting shockwave nearly knocks me to the ground.

Silence falls, punctuated by the occasional plop of falling sprinkles.

Cynric emerges from under the worktable. "Did we win?"

Marlena shucks frosting off her shirt. "Define 'win.'"

But the shop isn't done.

A burbling sound comes from the front. Racing to stop whatever might be happening there, I nearly step on Lady Wyndolynn, who jets for the staircase. I duck as a battalion of gumdrop missiles strafes the display case.

Torren is on my heels and skids to a stop at the case to shut down the revolt. The pretty chocolate fountain set up for Valentine's Day near the register erupts, spraying his left boot with enough dark cocoa to drown a leprechaun.

The floorboards tremble and begin to bulge upwards.

Hansel enters and slams his palm against them. "Root and stone, be *still!*"

Izzy leaps for a teetering jar on the shelf. "Not the sprinkles!"

Cynric scribbles on the back of a napkin, numbers glowing faintly blue as they rise into the air and dissipate. "Seraphina—is caramel viscosity at 180 degrees?"

"Brilliant!" I flick my wrist toward the industrial mixer in the back. The machine whirs to life, spewing thick amber ribbons that I direct to snare airborne jawbreakers. Torren mutters curses as he wrestles a sentient rolling pin that's rolled right into our midst.

Marlena tosses me a saltshaker. "Counterclockwise for hexes!"

"Unless it's a Class Three confection curse," Izzy says. "Then you'll need—"

"A dash of cinnamon," I finish, upending the shaker over a cluster of chocolate coins.

The wall sconces choose that moment to bust into glass shards. They fly at us. Flower, who's been entertaining herself in the front windows, screeches and disappears through the wall.

Hansel's crossbow twangs—Dradus looses a bolt wrapped in linen napkins. The projectile unfurls midair, becoming a fabric net that catches falling debris with the precision of a parachuting spiderweb.

A sudden quiet descends. None of us move. Seconds, then a minute, tick by.

Torren breaks the quiet, his jacket glazed in buttercream. "Status? Is anyone injured?"

We all claim to be okay.

Marlena prods a quivering mound of whipped cream with her shoe. "It's...singing."

The cream trembles, then launches into a pitchy rendition of *Somewhere Over the Rainbow*.

Hansel blinks. "Do we kill it?"

The cream stops mid-note. "Don't you dare," Izzy snaps, but then looks as if she doesn't have a better idea.

My ears ring. I lean against the candy-smeared counter, surveying the battlefield—walls glittering with hardened sugar, floorboards mosaicked in frosting, filling, and powdered sugar, Torren picking gumballs from his hair like some battle-weary king.

Izzy breaks first. Her snort sparks a chain reaction—Cynric's shoulders shake silently, Marlena's dignified snicker escapes through pressed lips, and even Torren's mouth twitches as he extracts a chocolate chip from under his collar.

Hansel holds out the longest. Then, the whipped cream busts out a high note.

"That's it." He collapses onto the floor, laughter rumbling deep as an earthquake. "Veramis sure knows how to cause chaos."

The brooch is still warm against my chest. "Look on the bright side. At least the floor's sealed now."

Cynric prods a floorboard with his shoe. "Adhesive rating... impressive."

I kick a stray jellybean and glance at my godmother. "Do we need a mop or a flamethrower?"

Torren examines his ruined boots. "Both, I believe."

Marlena waves the idea off and gestures for us to follow her to the back. There, she conjures a fresh tea tray with mismatched cups from my growing collection. A moment later, lavender vanilla steam curls around her smudged cheek as she winks at me and lifts her mug. "To containing catastrophes."

Our mugs clink. Outside, Enchanted Haven is bedded down for the night, oblivious to the carnage.

Hansel licks a smear of chocolate from his thumb. "So. We good to hunt evil witches now?"

The cream bursts out in a spectacular crescendo.

Izzy grins. "After the curtain call."

Chapter Ten

I'm barely awake the next morning as I stumble to the kitchen to get the oven going. Only two days until the festival, and all of my baked goods and candies were ruined last night.

Marlena and Izzy are equally tired. Morale is low. When opening time comes around, we barely have enough goodies to fill the case and no extras.

Mayor Jo enters the moment I flip the sign, his usually impeccable cowboy hat crooked. "Seraphina," he says, "the fountain in Whimsy Park just spat out sulfuric-smelling gas bubbles and a live trout."

I pause mid-swipe of my cleaning rag across the glass display case. "Trout?"

His fingers drum an uneven rhythm against the countertop. "First, Mrs. Pettigrew's prize roses started blooming already and singing sea shanties at midnight, then Tom Hunt's farm sign switched all his prices to dragon eggs, and now this?" He uses a napkin to wipe off the back of his neck. "We're two days from the Enchanted Hearts Festival. I can't have Main Street flooded with gas bubbles during the parade!"

Marlena enters from the back in jeans, wiping powdered sugar from her hands onto an apron embroidered with 'Witchin' Kitchen' in glittering thread. We've managed to clean the place from stem to stern and fix the broken wall sconces, but little else. "Mayor," she says, her calm voice soothing, "perhaps you'd like a—"

"Turnover?" he asks. "I'm going to need a dozen if this continues. Please tell me you've found the source of these glitches, Seraphina."

The truth lodges in my throat. The brooch, the charm—Veramis. Admitting what's going on might send him spiraling, especially if I can't figure out how to break the feedback loop or stop the evil queen.

I force a smile, putting the cleaning rag away and using tongs to grab a caramel. "We're working on it. All of us. Have a caramel."

"They're infused with chamomile and lavender," Marlena adds, plucking one for herself. "I'll pack up some turnovers for you."

Mayor Jo unwraps the candy with trembling fingers. "But the festival—"

"Will dazzle." I pat his hand and pour him a coffee to go. "Remember when the carousel ponies escaped during the New Year's mixer? We turned it into a pony painting fundraiser. Got six new statues for the park."

He chews slowly, shoulders losing their ear-level tension. "That Pegasus did look good in teal."

"Exactly. These glitches will die down." The lie tastes salty on my tongue. "Marlena and I will make sure nothing interferes with the festival."

Izzy ambles in, tugging Hansel with her. "Us, too. The festival is going to be wonderful."

Hansel stays silent for once, but I don't miss how his fingers are threaded through Izzy's.

Appeased, Mayor Jo snatches another caramel, the coffee, and the bag of treats. "Whatever you need, let me know. Torren and Cyn can help."

They already are, but I don't say that as I wave bye to him, and he leaves.

As the door clicks shut behind him, we all breathe a sigh of relief. It's short-lived.

The bell jangles, and Trinken barrels in, looking like he lost a fight with a tornado—hair full of twigs, one sleeve ripped at the shoulder, and smelling distinctly of faery dust. He collapses against the counter. "Ever After's locked down. All portals dead-end at a wall of thorns soaked in nightmare nettles."

Marlena stiffens. "Any word from the other side?"

"None." He accepts the caramel I offer him. "Good news is the blockade's fresh. Royal Intelligence must be onto Veramis's coup."

Hope sparks in my chest. "If the palace realizes she's gone rogue—"

"We can't depend on them for help," Hansel says. "We have to manage this ourselves. Izzy is undoubtedly our best way to subdue Veramis while we destroy her army."

Trinken groans and scratches at the rash spreading on his arm. "Why do overlords always go for dramatic vegetation? A simple 'Keep Out' sign would suffice."

"You are an Outcast," I remind him gently. "You're supposed to keep out."

"I know." He ruffles his hair, sending a cascade of twigs and leaves to the floor. "Do you need me to rally the troops?"

I've leaned on the Outcast community here more than once. They've always come through for me. "They'll get caught in the crossfire if Veramis succeeds. Ask for volunteers to help us keep her from taking over." I have to hope at least a few would join our cause. "We must protect our own, as well as the humans in this realm."

Outside, a group of giggling tourists pass by carrying star-shaped wish lanterns. Marlena slips a vial of anti-itch powder into Trinken's coat pocket as he leaves by the back exit.

But after a long day of baking and waiting on customers, I'm no closer to figuring out how to track down Gretel or stop Veramis. Hansel goes to the church to meet up with Torren and Cyn. Izzy helps out with the shop, discussing various ideas with Marlena and me between customers.

As the sun sets, Torren enters. Pine needles cling to his tailored coat, and a smear of something greenish across his cheek might be lichen. Behind him, Cyn brushes dirt from his sleeves.

But it's Hansel who cuts straight to my heart.

He stomps straight to the pastry case and leans on it like it's the only thing keeping him upright. His soil-stained fingers leave smudges on the glass, and his collar is torn.

When our eyes meet, his mouth twists into something that's not quite a smile. "We covered every path, every meadow, every tree," he rasps once I get all three in the back room and shove mugs of spiced cocoa at them. "We followed every trail, checked every hollow. Even the blue jays stopped responding to my whistles after the seventh mile."

Cyn perches on a stool, wiping his mouth with the back of his hand. "We found seven abandoned campsites, twelve suspicious moss patches, and a very confused badger wearing a hat. But no sign of Gretel or Veramis anywhere."

Hansel's knuckles whiten around his mug. "I thought for sure the winged ones would find her and report back."

Torren plucks a truffle from the parchment-lined work-table, inspecting it like a general surveying a battle plan. "If Veramis has half the cunning you claim,"—he pops the chocolate in his mouth, speaking around the ganache filling—"she's still watching you, Seraphina. We need to change tactics. Maybe we should be trying to draw her here. To you. To Izzy."

I've been thinking the same thing all day. It was Marlena's idea and it scares me, but it might be the only way.

The shop's usual warmth feels suddenly stifling. I'm reaching for the broom to sweep up imaginary crumbs when the temperature drops sharply. Frost patterns bloom over the display windows as Flower materializes upside-down above the worktable, her translucent flared-leg denim pants sliding to reveal her pale calves.

"Oh good, you're all here!" Her voice echoes as if coming from the bottom of a well. "I followed the most delightful woodchuck! It had cheeks like overstuffed handbags and kept reciting limericks about turnips!"

I let the others know she's joined us. Marlena mutters an incantation so they can see and hear her again.

"Feeling better?" Izzy asks.

"Much." Flower rights herself with a spin. "Is your friend a soldier? I saw a bunch of those. They looked ever so grumpy, all lined up in the dark with their ugly clay faces. They make this weird noise, too, like, well, ghosts in cartoons. *Woooo*," she imitates, raising her hands. "Except the one missing its nose—that one seemed more shocked than grumpy."

Hansel's mug clatters against the table. "Where?"

"East bluffs, the third cave from the screeching owl tree." Flower twirls a strand of spectral hair around her finger. "Though I might've gotten distracted counting quartz veins in the—"

I'm already untying my apron strings and gathering my own army of candies. "Show me."

Marlena grabs Gunther from the hook near the back door. "Show *us*. You'll need reinforcements."

"No." The word comes out sharper than I intend. "If this is a Veramis trap, I won't risk anyone. But..." My gaze flicks to Hansel's clenched jaw. "...I could use someone who knows how to find family with good old common sense."

He's halfway to the door before I finish speaking.

They all ignore me. Closing procedures happen in a blur. Through the front windows, I see Hansel pacing beneath the lamppost crowned with wish lanterns, his shadow stretching long across the cobblestones.

"This requires stealth," Torren says as we all pile out to join Hansel. "I'll scout ahead."

Cyn pushes between us, a living barrier of werewolf once he shifts. "I'm the one with the nose. Stick to brooding in the shadows, Count Cocoa Puff."

Hansel's voice slices through the banter. "We're wasting moonlight."

We hurry into the indigo evening, Hansel glancing at the tree line where fireflies mimic distant lanterns. "The wood thrushes promised to keep searching," he mutters, more to the night than to me.

Flower drifts ahead, her glow casting moonbeam puddles on the path. "Oh, I do hope we meet that woodchuck again—he owed me a punchline about parsnips."

"Everyone, take one of these." I hand out anti-curse lollipops. They sparkle under the streetlights. "Suck, don't crunch. The spell lasts longer that way."

Cyn snorts as I stick one in his toothy maw. "If I die because a witch mistook me for a sparkly toothpick," he says in his guttural wolf voice around the lollipop, "I'm haunting you first."

"Too late," Flower sings. "Haunting positions are *very* competitive these days."

I click my tongue, our motley crew picking up our speed on our race to the cliffs. Torren sticks as close as my shadow, Cyn zips ahead to sniff every leaf and rock, and Hansel loosens his crossbow. Marlena keeps a ready hand on Gunther's hilt. My chest warms despite the danger coiling in the air. These aren't just allies. They're the family I've cobbled together.

The scent of crisp night air and pine trees sharpens the twilight as we leave Enchanted Haven's cottages behind. The forest path is narrow and dark, bracken crunching underfoot. Marlena forms a witch light to illuminate the trail, and Torren helps me over a fallen log, barely disturbing the ferns.

Flower twirls ahead, humming a nursery rhyme that changes key every third note. "Next left," she says, but I already know the route. I fought kobolds—magical creatures from Ever After—at the bluffs.

"Does anyone else taste static?" Izzy asks. "Like licking a storm cloud?"

A chorus of caws shatters the night. Six crows, black as licorice drops, swoop low over our heads. Their feathers shimmer faintly purple at the tips—Veramis's signature hue. Instead of attacking as I expect, they perch on a giant, gnarled tree, tilting their heads in unison.

Hansel freezes. "Trap?"

"Invitation," I murmur. The largest crow drops something at my feet—a maple leaf veined with gold. Recognition prickles my scalp. "Gretel used these as trail markers when we used to hike in the woods."

Hansel eyes the leaf. "Maybe they know where she is."

Cyn squints. "Since when do murder birds play tour guide?"

"Since never." Torren takes the leaf and sniffs it. "I sense no magic." He glances at me. "Do you?"

No, but it's still a sign. "If the crows are helping her, the leaf doesn't need to be enchanted."

The birds take flight, leading us deeper into the woods. We follow, our footfalls syncing with the rhythm of distant frog songs. Odd they would be active this time of year. A few random and obviously magical fireflies wink in code across dead-leafed bushes, and I catch Flower trying to high-five one.

"Stay sharp," Marlena whispers. "Veramis plants traps like dandelions."

Flower passes through an outcropping of boulders, reemerging with a gasp. "There's a badger wedding inside! Complete with acorn confetti!" She blinks. "Wait, was I supposed to scout? Oops."

A twig snaps. We spin as one—everyone ready to fight. The underbrush rustles, revealing a hedgehog rolling a hazelnut. Its beady eyes judge us before waddling away.

We continue on. The trees thin, revealing cliffs that bite into the horizon. Wind howls through fissures in the stone, carrying whispers that raise the hairs on my neck. The crows circle above a yawning cave mouth before dissolving into violet smoke. Below them, the ground slopes unnaturally smooth— no pebbles, no weeds, just packed dirt gleaming faintly wet under the stars. In the distance, the river gurgles.

Torren kneels, pressing a palm to the earth. "Bloodroot. Wolfsbane. Grave mold." His nose wrinkles. "This soil's been hexed."

Cyn shifts into his human form. "I can smell it."

Hansel crouches beside a half-buried clay shard, running

his thumb over its grooved surface. "This is from a kiln-fired armor plate."

Flower floats toward the entrance, spectral glow dimming with every inch. I want to call her back, fearing she might alert Veramis or get herself into trouble again.

Marlena cups my shoulder. Near the cave's dimly lit edge, seven twisted saplings form a perfect circle. Their branches coil inward, glistening with something darker than dew. My stomach churns.

"Hansel?" I nod toward the trees. "Are those...?"

"Blood oaks." He unslings his bow, face grim. "Gretel burned one once. Screamed for hours after."

Torren peers into the gloom, eyes reflecting crimson. "Someone reshaped the land itself here."

The cave exhales rot-scented air. Somewhere in that darkness, answers wait—about Veramis, Gretel, and the curse that made me and everyone I know believe I killed Izzy.

Hansel's shoulder brushes mine. "You stay with Izzy. Let us handle this."

"Oh, no," I say. "Izzy and I are just as capable of handling ourselves in battle as you are."

She sidles up on my other side, linking her arm through mine. She's sucking on her lollipop and removes to say, "This is my fight as much as it is yours, Hansel."

"I wish you to stay safe," he counters.

"You worry about yourself," she orders in her commanding princess voice.

Torren catches Hansel's eye. "I'll cover them."

I fight not to roll my eyes. No matter what we say, they view us as damsels in need of protection.

The cave walls press closer with every step, lichen

squelching underfoot. Marlena freezes ahead of me. "That's not possible," she whispers.

I nudge past her and nearly drop my sack of enchanted candies.

They stand in perfect ranks—hundreds of clay figures taller than Hansel, their hollow eye sockets studded with jagged amethyst shards. The witch light glints off their jointed limbs, casting jittery shadows that make their fingers twitch. The air smells of burnt pottery.

Hansel runs his palm over a soldier's cracked shoulder plate. "Not all of these are fresh. Some are centuries old."

Onyx heats suddenly, and I gasp. "Something's here. Watching us."

We all jump as the nearest soldier's head creaks toward the sound of my voice. For a heartbeat, nothing moves. Then, the amethyst eyes begin pulsing.

"Not good," Marlena says, jerking Gunther out of her belt.

Torren snatches my hand. "Time for a strategic retreat!"

We're halfway to the entrance when my pendant breaks free from under my jacket, yanked toward the cave's heart by invisible strings. I glimpse a large stone embedded in the farthest wall in the shape of a crow before Torren drags me into the cloudy night.

Breathless, I press Onyx back down under my jacket as we race down the path, but the gargoyle pops up, pointing toward those waiting clay soldiers. Is Gretel hidden inside? I pull up sharply. "Wait. We have to go back. Gretel may be in there."

The males exchange a glance. Torren lifts me, fireman style, and tosses me over his shoulder. To Cyn and Hansel, he says, "You go check. I'll take them home."

Before I can protest, he takes off running through the woods with me. Izzy and Marlena follow close on his heels.

Chapter Eleven

The path blurs beneath me as Torren's shoulder digs into my ribs with every hurried step. His grip is tight. "Put me down, vampyre," I command. "We're not done at the cave!"

He doesn't break stride. "Safety first. Your heroic streak's going to get you into trouble."

My fingers are already in my pocket, closing around a lemon drop. The candy buzzes against my palm, its magic a fizzy promise. "You know what really stinks?" I say sweetly, twisting to meet his glittering dark gaze. "When someone underestimates me."

He opens his mouth to respond and I drop the candy onto his tongue before he can blink.

"Stop and put me down," I say.

He halts mid-step, boots scraping against stone. His throat works once—a swallow that sounds almost offended—and suddenly, I'm sliding down his body like a sack of flour. My feet hit the pavement as he stiffens, shoulders rigid.

His voice comes out syrupy and slow. "Did...you...just...?"

"I sure did." I've used these to force him to do my bidding

before. Do I feel guilty? A little, but I straighten my skirt and pat his cheek. "Three minutes of obedient zombie. Plenty of time to march your fancy boots back to that cave and—"

"Seraphina!"

Flower materializes from between two storefronts. Something that resembles dandelion fluff escapes her braid as she jabs a finger toward Whimsy Park. "The weeping willow by the duck pond! The crows are congregating there."

Hansel steps into the streetlight's glow, crossbow strapped to his back. Cyn is with him. "We could find no trace of Gretel at the cave."

Why did Onyx react so, then? Was it some spell by Veramis to distract us? "To Whimsy Park," I say. "Let's find those crows."

A minute later, the crunch of frost-tipped grass keeps us company as we spill into the park. My breath hangs in milky puffs, the cold nipping at my fingertips. Above us, clouds swallow the moon, leaving the duck pond's surface polished black. Torren says nothing, yet his silence speaks volumes—he's mad as a hornet over my use of the lemon drop.

"There!" Flower pirouettes as she points to one of several willows. "I love how it dances with the wind!"

The tree hulks at the water's edge, branches clattering and reminding me of Ms. Nyssa's bone accessories. Every other tree stands still.

Hansel thumbs the strap of his crossbow. "I see no crows."

Cyn sniffs the air. "Smells like magic."

Izzy catches my sleeve. She tilts her head, curls spilling over her scarf. "There's a hum." Her eyes widen, pupils swallowing the scant starlight. "Like flies trapped in a music box."

Marlena comes up beside me. "Another trap or a dead end?"

We approach in wary formation—Flower skipping ahead, Torren's aggravated silence behind me, Izzy clutching my elbow. Hansel peels off to my left, Cynric to my right.

The willow's trunk twists, revealing bark split in silvery fissures. Onyx heats on my collarbone.

Danger.

Something wet plops onto my cheek.

"Great." I swipe at it. "Just what we need—rain."

"Crows," Marlena corrects.

The murder descends in a feathered cyclone, perching among the rattling branches. The largest pecks at a twig until it snaps, the splinter landing at my feet like a dare.

"Signs and portents," Marlena says drily. "How original."

Torren breaks his silence when I edge closer to the tree. His protective magic tickles my own. "Risky behavior, Princess."

"Shh." I press a palm to the trunk. The bark tickles, the vibrations climbing my arm and settling behind my molars with the tang of forbidden magic.

"Can you hear it?" Izzy whispers.

Hear it, feel it, hate it. Yes, the black magic makes my stomach roil and my head pound.

Hansel nocks an arrow. "Back up, Seraphina."

"Wait." My fingernails catch on a crevice oozing sap. "This could be it. This tree is—"

The ground lurches.

Torren's hands clamp around my waist, yanking me sideways as roots erupt from beneath me. We crash into Cyn, and the three of us go down, Torren's body cushioning my fall. Above us, the willow shudders, shedding crows and sticks in equal measure.

Marlena waves her sword. "Shall I kill it?"

"No," I wheeze, extracting an elbow from Torren's ribs.

The tree's vibrations race through my bones, insistent. "It's not attacking. It's humming."

Flower claps. "Told you!"

Izzy scrambles forward and presses both palms to the trunk. "That's it! A message," she breathes. "A song. But the melody's inverted. Like taffy spun backward through the puller."

Hansel lowers his crossbow an inch. "Explain without confectionery metaphors."

Marlena jabs Gunther's tip into sap—it sizzles. "Someone bottled a spell inside this glorified toothpick. It's fighting back."

Cyn and Torren gain their feet and flank me. The crows begin crooning, a cacophony that resolves into disturbingly human whispers. Onyx vibrates against my skin, searing heat spreading along my collarbone.

Torren scans the tree. "What type of spell?"

"Good question," I say. "It feels like black magic to me."

He eyes me like I'm a naughty child in need of discipline. "Is there a way to bind it without putting yourself in danger?"

"Possibly. Izzy, do you sense any weak points?"

Her hands skate over the bark. "Here." She taps a knot shaped like a keyhole. "The song is weakest here. If we can reverse it, make the tree hum like it should, maybe we can break the spell."

Marlena sighs. "If you get turned into a topiary, I'm selling the shop to Trinken's wife."

The crows fall silent as I press strings of licorice into the knot. Somewhere beyond the pond, a church bell chimes the witching hour. *"Threads of sweetness snag the rhyme. Turn it back to its rightful beat and time."*

The candy melts into the bark, and a deep sigh vibrates up

my arm—not the harsh buzz of before, but the resonant beat of a drum deep underground.

Izzy presses her ear to the trunk. "I hear a heartbeat," she says.

Marlena squints at the gnarled roots. "If this goes wrong, we could end up joining it."

The bark splits with a crack. Torren snatches me again, yanking me back. A deep hollow yawns open at the base of the trunk, exhaling air that smells of damp earth. Hansel points his crossbow at it.

I grip a handful of candies, ready to throw them at anything that appears or attacks.

Nothing does.

Izzy tugs my sleeve. "Leftmost shadow," she whispers. "It's breathing."

I nearly drop the candies. Beneath the tree's twisted roots, a patch of darkness pulses. "Stand back," I warn, picking out a gummy bear and a gumball and binding them with a licorice whip. Cold blasts outward from the combo as I mutter another incantation, crystallizing spiderwebs into lace necklaces. The dark patch shivers, revealing—

"Holy sugarplums," I whisper.

Gretel lies curled like a napping hedgehog, her chestnut braids tangled with oak leaves. Izzy crouches, hands hovering over Gretel's dirty red cloak. "Enchantment residue," she murmurs.

Hansel's arrow tip dips, and he reaches for his sister with one hand. "How do we wake her?"

"Wait." I kneel next to the hollow and touch her skin. It feels suspiciously room-temperature but is a sickly gray. "Sleeping beauty spell," I tell them. The earlier cell phone symphony now makes sense.

Torren shakes off the last effects of the lemon drop. "Seven minutes," he announces, checking his watch. "If that long."

"'Til what?" Cyn asks.

"Until whatever put her there comes for us. Undoubtedly, the crows have already alerted our evil queen that we are here."

Hansel shakes Gretel's arm. "Wake up, sister. Now!"

My gaze flicks over Gretel's leaf-strewn hair. Somewhere overhead, the crows begin their eerie whispering chorus again. Flower hovers closer, peering at Gretel and then up where the crows watch. "It's nice that whoever put your friend down there didn't want her to be alone."

Nice, *right*. "Everyone be ready to fight or run," I order, grabbing a lemon drop. "If this goes sideways, those will be our only options."

Chapter Twelve

"Come on, Gretel," I whisper, pressing the lemon drop past her lips. I pause a moment and then say, "I command you to wake up."

It dissolves into liquid gold. Her skin grows warmer under my palm, the gray pallor retreating. Her lashes lift, revealing eyes the deep green of pine needles after rain.

Hansel cheers, and the vise around my ribs loosens.

"Welcome back," I say as I tug a leaf from her hair. "We've missed you, and you owe us an explanation."

She blinks at me, then snorts—a rough, wonderful sound. "Owe you? Charging for life-saving services now, Princess?" The playful jab dies as she pushes herself upright, her brother lending a hand. "Veramis. She's plotting—" She grimaces and grabs her neck, massaging a kink from it.

"To take over this world and Ever After?" I finish. "We figured that out."

She grabs her bow, accepts Hansel's assistance, and steps out of the hollow, cradling it. "She's built an army. I was tracking her movements, and then..." Her gaze goes fuzzy. "And then..."

"She put a sleeping spell on you."

Gretel glances at Cynric and Torren, confusion knitting her brow. "I don't know them. Do I?" she adds.

Hansel grabs her up in a bear hug. "Thank the kingdom you're alive!"

Gretel pats his arm, encouraging him to put her down. She digs a thumb under her leather bracer, producing a folded parchment that she hands to me. "It's the proof your mother wanted. Veramis has been siphoning magic from this realm's ley lines and feeding it to..." She shudders, hands curling into fists. "Creatures. Not golems, not constructs. They *breathe*. They're somewhat sentient. She calls them shadow ghouls."

Marlena's silver-streaked hair catches the breeze as she rubs the handle of her sword. "Veramis can't sustain such dark magic long-term."

"She can if she has the brooch." I touch the empty spot on my cloak where Mother's heirloom should rest someday when I become queen. Which I never will. "The royal jewelry has been crafted with royal blood. She needs that blood to control the flow of magic from the ley lines to feed to her soldiers."

Gretel nods. "Your blood would do just as well as the brooch. Veramis traded the piece to a witch named—"

"Cambria," Torren supplies. "We're aware."

Gretel frowns. "And who are you?"

I do a quick round of introductions.

"She'll come to the shop," Izzy says quietly, hovering near a hawthorn bush.

Gretel whirls, causing her bow to clatter to the ground. "Isadora Ravenswood. You're supposed to be dead." Her shocked expression turns on me. "You killed her."

Izzy peers at her own palms as though checking for transparency. "Apparently not."

I catch Izzy's wrist before she can retreat into the shadows. "Veramis staged the murder and enchanted us all. Made me see an alternate version of what really happened." The phantom scent of burnt hair and clothes floods my nose, the memory too much to bear, even though I know it isn't real. I focus on Izzy's pulse thrumming under my thumb, steady as a metronome. "Izzy is alive, and we have much to tell you. Veramis is now focused on creating an alternate version of this reality."

Torren's boot snaps one of the fallen branches, his eyes scanning the park for enemies. "As heartwarming as this reunion is, perhaps we should discuss all this in a safer location?"

Marlena plucks the parchment from my grip. "This goes to Queen Lethia, yes?" she asks Gretel. "I'll have it delivered before dawn."

"Wait." Gretel staggers forward. "Veramis' creatures—I think they're vulnerable to iron. Tell the queen to mobilize the blacksmiths."

Somewhere beyond the trees, Enchanted Haven's clock-tower chimes. Didn't I just hear a church bell telling me it was midnight? The sound echoes around us, time and space warping.

Cyn lifts his sensitive nose to the wind. "Something's coming. Half-mile back or so, but moving fast."

"The shadow ghouls," Gretel says.

Torren also sniffs the air. "It's the same scent we picked up on in the cave."

Izzy takes my hand. "So, we're running, right? Like, now?"

The tremor hits like a giant's footfall. The branches on the ground dance across the forest floor. Torren grabs my arm.

Gretel snatches a bow from Hansel's stash and aims toward the approaching attackers. "We stand."

"We run," I counter. "No telling what tricks Veramis still has for us."

Hansel yanks Gretel's bow from her hands and catches her around the waist, lifting her in the air once more. "Quickly."

Torren tugs me along at a breakneck speed. I keep a firm grip on Izzy.

Our pursuers sound less like soldiers and more like an avalanche—snarling throats, splintering saplings, and the wet crackle of corrupted magic.

Gretel beats at her brother's chest. "This is idiocy! We're more effective as a team when planted!"

Torren vaults over a rotting log, his magic lifting Izzy and me over it with ease. "They're herding us northeast. Trying to cut off our path back to Main Street."

Gretel wrenches free of Hansel, landing with her boots in the loam. "I refuse to run!"

Hansel keeps her bow out of reach, holding it over his head. "My arrows will not stop them!"

"We have to try."

Marlena sighs. "Family reunions are so heartwarming."

A shadow ghoul lunges from the bracken—all red clay that looks like armor. Torren intercepts it mid-leap, his fangs sinking into the creature's throat with a wet crunch. They fall to the ground. The taste must be foul; he leaps up and spits out a mouthful of dirt.

While the attack slowed the creature, it does not pause for long, roaring into the night and lunging for us again.

Gretel jerks the arrow from Hansel, and her bow magically appears in her hands. As another beast swipes at Izzy, her arrow takes it through the eye socket.

Three more crest the ridge.

Hansel shouts, "We're not going to make it."

"Fine!" I snap. "New plan."

"Finally!" Gretel nocks another arrow.

Not hers, mine. "We run *faster*."

Another tremor. Closer this time. The shadow ghouls howl in unison—a sound that turns my insides to jelly.

Cyn's canines flash as he shifts. "They're calling reinforcements!"

We plunge downhill toward the creek, our reflections fracturing in the calm water. Behind us, the shadow ghouls' guttural snarls rip through the night.

Gretel stops and lays down her bow. "Stand. Your. Ground! We'll dig a trench."

Hansel grunts in resignation, kneeling. "We root here."

"You better dig a trench deeper than your ego," Izzy shouts.

Cyn spins toward the tree line. "Here comes the next wave."

The shadow ghouls burst through the pines, glowing with amethyst eyes.

My throat tightens as Torren places himself in front of me like a shield. Marlena joins him, and I can barely see over the wall they've formed. "Are you sure this will work?" I call to the twins.

"Now!" Gretel barks.

They slam their palms to the ground in unison. The earth buckles, and I stumble into Torren as fissures spiderweb across the ground under us.

"Brace!" Hansel growls through gritted teeth.

The world splits open with a groan that vibrates my molars. A chasm yawns wide beneath the charging soldiers, swallowing their hisses and cries whole. Dirt cascades into the void, and one clawed hand grasps the crumbling edge before Gretel smashes her booted foot down on it.

In the next instant, the earth seals shut with a finality that reminds me of Mother's vault in Ever After.

Silence crashes over us, broken only by Izzy's shaky giggle. "Well. That's one way to make a grave."

Gretel sags against Hansel, her breathing ragged.

"Is everyone still in one piece?" I ask.

A chorus of exhausted affirmations echoes around me. Torren tugs me toward home. "That bought us five minutes. Tops."

The creek gurgles, carrying away flecks of dark magic that sizzle against the stones. Hansel claps dirt from his hands. "Shop's warded. We fortify there."

I help Gretel up, her calloused fingers squeezing mine. "They're not just in the bluffs," she says. "I think Veramis planted some in the town's roots. Waiting."

"Dormant death squads. Have to hand it to her, she's strategic."

Marlena scans the area. "We're going to need to fortify the town. Double-layered protection spells. Magical barriers at the sewer grates. Someone needs to watch The Witching Well."

"Barriers won't be any good if they're already inside the spell lattice," Hansel says.

Marlena kicks a pebble, sending it skittering into the underbrush as she gripes at me. "You should've let me install those chocolate-coated landmines at Solstice."

Gretel's chuckle turns into a cough. "Remember when Ambrosia enchanted lollipops to sing battle hymns?"

I wince at the memory. "Let's keep that one to ourselves. And it's Seraphina now. That's who I am here."

Hansel keeps looking over his shoulder. "Priorities. We need someone in the clock tower. It's the best vantage point."

"Already covered." Cyn flashes his teeth. "I recruited a few of my parishioners to keep an eye on the whole town."

Gretel stumbles, her knee buckling. I catch her elbow, surprised by how cold her skin feels. "Swap," I tell Hansel, ducking under her other arm.

"Still bossy," she grumbles.

"And you're still stubborn."

The cheerful shop windows glow under the street lights. Our footsteps slow in unison, and we duck inside.

If only we were safe.

Chapter Thirteen

The sharp tang of worry replaces The Candy Cauldron's usual vanilla and sugar-scented calm. My friends cluster around the worktable—Cynric's fingers drumming an uneven rhythm on the top and Torren's unnatural stillness making the glitter in his dark eyes look frostbitten.

I worry my pendant. "Veramis wants the whole town as her personal chessboard, and we're the pawns. If she can take over Enchanted Haven and control the ley lines, she'll keep expanding her authority until she commands a big enough army to defeat my parents."

Gretel snaps a Valentine's cookie in half. "Then we flip the board." Next to her, Hansel nods, fingers already tracing invisible battle formations on the table.

Torren rises smoothly, his velvet coat whispering as he leans over the map of Enchanted Haven spread between jars of hot cinnamon candies. "Pawns become queens if they defeat evil." His smile is all fang and flirtation, but the strategy he goes on to sketch out is ruthlessly precise. "Cyn already has the clock tower covered. We need more supernaturals to watch all those coming and going at the festival. Do perimeter sweeps. Have blockades ready for the shadow ghouls. We also need to figure out an effective way to destroy them. Burying them worked this time, but what if Veramis raises them? What if she can make more with a flourish of her wand?"

Cynric grunts. "My pack can handle the perimeter sweeps. We'll scent dark magic before it crosses the creek."

A knock on the back door makes all of us jump. Cyn sniffs the air. "It's all right," he says. "The angel is here."

Torren lets Mayor Jo in. "Seraphina, the festival committee is demanding six more cases of heart-shaped truffles." He freezes, taking in the war council crowded into the small room. "Oh. Hello."

I motion him to join us. "Mayor Jo, meet my friends Hansel and Gretel."

To his credit, he only hesitates a second before shaking their hands and welcoming them to town. "I've seen you around," he says to Hansel, "with Cyn and Torren." His scrutiny falls on me. "How bad is it?"

Not much gets past him. Marlena hands him a piece of fudge. "You better sit."

He does, and between all of us, we explain who Veramis is, what she's planning, and our recent encounter with her ghoul army.

He swallows the fudge in a single bite. "How many soldiers are we talking about? Do they prefer direct attacks or psychological warfare?"

Hansel leans on the table's edge, his heavy frame making it creak. "We don't know the extent of their numbers, but they are foot soldiers. Somewhat sentient, but under the queen's command and control. Direct attacks from them. More psychological from her." He glances at Izzy.

The mayor looks sick but squares his shoulders. "I'll mobilize the neighborhood watch. Mrs. Peppercorn's book club has been itching for something more exciting than debating vampyre romance novels."

Torren coughs. "That could put them in more danger than it would do good."

Mayor Jo comes to his feet. "I must call an emergency council meeting. They won't be happy at this early morning hour, but this can't wait."

He leaves, and Hansel and Torren assign us our roles.

I hand out what candy I have left that might assist everyone should they find themselves in trouble. Then, I start gathering ingredients to make more.

Hansel and Gretel head out, arguing about trap placements. Through the shop window, I watch them pause beneath the enchanted streetlamps. Hansel kneels, palms flat on cobblestones as roots punch through cracks to weave thorny lattices over the street grates. Gretel spins her arrow tip in a slow circle, every shop's flower boxes bursting into violent bloom—roses with teeth, snapdragons that hiss.

Marlena hums off-key as she levitates jars of flour, sugar, and molasses off high shelves. We're all tired and sore, but there's work to be done.

"Citrus Burst gumdrops," I tell her, wiggling my fingers for her to send the sugar my way.

She flicks a finger without looking. The jar floats behind her and over to me. She's mastered this world's physics and enjoys using her magic without much repercussion now. I fear if she overdoes it, however, she'll end up with a migraine that rivals Izzy's.

Izzy has gone upstairs to lie down, overcome with weariness and the realization that it might be up to her and me to stop her mother's evil plans.

I melt pink sugar crystals with lemon zest, adding a small dose of my magic before I pour the concoction into molds. "We need more fudge, too. I never got Tina Metcalf's mint chocolate order done."

"Make a double batch, and we'll use a pound of it as a truth serum. I might feed one to you so you'll admit where you hid my good throwing stars."

A snort escapes me. "They're in the false bottom of the flour bin. I only hid them because the ghost boy kept playing with them."

Within the hour, we have plenty of fudge, chocolate truffles, butterscotch candies, and gumballs wrapped in special paper or packed in our glass jars. Our candy hearts with messages are restocked, too. I've used a normal amount of magic, but because I'm so tired, even that feels like a monumental task. "Three orders down, backup weapon candies made, and now we can focus on some treats for the festival."

"Four down," Marlena corrects, showing me a tray of marzipan hearts. "I had an emergency stash of these under the display case bottom."

Smart. "Why do you think Veramis hasn't attacked me outright to get my blood?" I ask her. The thought has been tumbling around my mind all night.

Izzy stumbles in, clutching her temples, obsidian eyes gone cloudy. "I told Mother we're ready," she announces to a jar of sprinkles. "She said she'd be here soon. Unless she uses the... the thing with the..." Her sentence unravels as she blinks at Marlena.

I catch her elbow before she faceplants into the sink. "Easy, Princess. Why don't you sit?"

"No!" She jerks away, wild gaze finding mine. "This ends now. Even if she hates me." A shudder racks her frame. Her whisper comes out fractured. "Do you think there's still chocolate cake in the Ever After palace kitchens? Real buttercream, the kind that melts on your tongue like..."

Marlena slides a honeycomb lozenge into Izzy's palm. "Memory's slippery when chased. Best to let it come nibbling."

The princess crunches down. Her wince turns to wonder as golden light leaks between her teeth. "Oh! The fountain! We need the chocolate warm—wait, no, that's not..." She sags into a chair. "Why does remembering hurt?"

Torren's voice rumbles through the room as he materializes. "Have you truly spoken with Queen Veramis, Isadora?"

She squints at him. "What?"

I get her some water. "You said you spoke to Mother, and she would be here soon."

"I did?"

I shake my head at Marlena and Torren. "It was most likely a dream or a hallucination. Ms. Nyssa's tonic has worn off."

Torren frowns, surveying the refilled jars on the shelves. "Have you weaponized enough confections?"

"A few." I toss him a molasses bomb. "Sticky situation insurance."

Cynric comes through the back door, the first tinge of sunrise on his heels. He snags a cocoa-dusted truffle from the display case. "Will these work against shadow magic, or are we just giving Veramis' minions diabetes?"

Before I can answer, Izzy lurches forward. "The black carriages," she gasps, fingers clawing at empty air. "With the screaming wheels. They came through the mirror. Mother's wearing Father's crown and laughing." Her knees buckle.

Marlena catches her, steering the shaking princess back onto the chair. "Breathe, child."

As Torren and Cyn discuss optimal ambush coordinates, my gaze snags on the vial of our private stash of Chamomile Sleep Tonic stuck behind the vanilla extract. I once discussed my recipe with Ms. Nyssa, but the kind she sells has a thick, distinct lavender undertone she swears by. It also has moth wings.

That's what Veramis used on Gretel; I'd bet my apron on it.

"The sleeping draught used on Gretel," I say. "Nyssa adds crushed moth wings to hers."

"And too much of that can place a person into a coma," Marlena adds.

Cynric growls. "Our potion mistress is playing both sides?"

"Or being played." Torren's thumb rubs along the edge of his jaw. "Shall I interrogate her?"

Izzy lifts her head, cheeks regaining some color. "Let me talk to her. If anyone understands my mother's manipulation, it's me."

"Absolutely not." I hang up my apron. "I'll handle Nyssa."

"She doesn't open until ten," Marlena says. "And I won't allow you to go off to challenge that witch without me. Remember what happened last time?" She points a finger at Izzy. "No more playing with mirrors or sleeping in case your mother is still manipulating you and plans to ambush us. Get yourself some coffee and make pastries." The finger shifts to point at me. "Retrieve my throwing stars from your hiding place. We may need them."

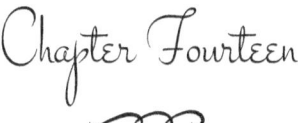

Chapter Fourteen

A trio of city workers argue over the proper Cupid arrow placement on the Witching Well's upper beam, their voices rising over the accordion music spilling from the tea shop as Torren, Marlena, and I head for Ms. Nyssa's.

I sidestep Maude, hustling to her office, and she's so distracted she doesn't even comment about my teeth. While avoiding her, I trip over Mrs. Peabody's corgi brigade. All six dogs sport tiny red bow ties that match their owner's feathered hat.

"Careful, dearie!" The woman adjusts her spectacles. "Bartholomew's small but mighty." The dog bears his teeth at me. I smile, adding a bit extra in a playful snarl back.

The spicy aroma hits me three blocks from the apothecary. My fingers brush the hot cinnamon candies in my pocket. Through Nyssa's bay window, dried mandrake roots bob in murky jars. A neon sign flickers: *Love Potions 25% Off – While Supplies Last!*

My reflection in the shop's glass door shows confidence I

don't feel. Maybe it's the anger in my belly causing my shoulders to square and hardening my features.

"Welcome!" Ms. Nyssa pops up from behind her counter at our entrance, her smile faltering when she sees it's me. Marlena keeps a few feet back, and Torren has made himself invisible. "You again." Her nails flutter toward the display of "Eternal Devotion" elixirs. "I don't suppose you're here for a love potion?"

I pluck a vial of dream root extract from the nearest shelf. "I want to discuss sleep aids." The glass warms in my palm, pulsing faintly. "Specifically, your specialty blend. The one with moth wings."

The lights flicker. So does something behind her eyes. "Oh?" Her forced laugh chips away at the silence, and although her head doesn't move, the bone beads in her hair clack. "Trouble sleeping?"

"I'm curious why Queen Veramis chose your signature recipe to sedate my friend and why you lied about it."

A fern on the checkout counter shrivels. Several of Nyssa's braids unravel, chestnut strands escaping to frame her suddenly ashen face. She busies herself rearranging already-alphabetized vials. "I didn't lie." She dismisses this new lie with a hand. "Clients pay for discretion. I have no idea who Queen Veramis is or why the woman who came to me five days ago wanted my potion, but trade secrets and all that."

"Discretion?" I laugh, a bitter sound that fills the shop's herbal air. I step closer, the floorboard creaking a warning. The cinnamons vibrate in my pocket. "Did she threaten you? Your supply lines? Or was it blackmail?"

Nyssa's gaze flicks to a closed door at the far end of the shop. Something thumps behind it—once, twice—before falling silent. "Some storms," she whispers, tracing a scar along her collarbone, "drown you faster than others."

Marlena unsheathes her sword. "Then you best find a strong shelter."

The woman seems to understand that we're her only hope of surviving the storm she's trying to ride out. "She took my niece." Her voice cracks, and she grabs a mortar and pestle, the scent of thyme and orris root clouding my senses as she grinds the leaves. "Said she'd make the girl into a living statue for her throne room."

Such a horrible queen. "Veramis is planning to take over our town," I inform her. "Your assistance with her plan makes you a traitor to all of us. You've forfeited any help me and my family might offer in getting your niece back."

Her pestle freezes mid-grind. "I know you're different, but I have no idea what kind of witch you genuinely are, nor do I know anything about any traitorous plans. All I did was try to keep someone I love safe."

"And that's what I'm trying to do, too."

"She's powerful. More so than you or me." She rubs the back of her hand under her nose. "I don't know what to do."

"You can start by telling us the truth," Marlena says, pointing the tip of Gunther at Nyssa's throat. "All of it."

She starts to retort, and Torren materializes right behind her. He grabs her wrist just as she's about to toss the ground herbs at us. "Think carefully about who you want to enrage at this moment," he says, holding her immobile as he speaks in her ear. His fangs are showing. "If you wish to survive the day, you best choose wisely."

The vampyre is ready to sink his fangs into her carotid. Marlena is ready to run the blade through her throat. She visibly swallows. The seconds tick by.

Another swallow makes the muscles in her neck work. "I'll tell you everything."

And she does.

"The shadow soldiers," she whispers. "They're fueled by the ley lines and something else, but they're bound by the jewels from Veramis' crown. Expose them to juniper smoke, and the binding will unravel."

I pluck a bundle of dried juniper from her hanging herbs. "Like breaking a sugar lattice with lemon juice."

Torren releases his deadly holds on the woman. Marlena lowers Gunther.

Nyssa lunges toward me. "You can't tell anyone I told you. If she finds out—"

Both of my bodyguards snag her and force her back.

"Help us stop her," I say. "Convert your rain spells into juniper mist machines. Or concoct potions with juniper smoke to throw at the soldiers. We may not need them, but if we do, you must make amends for your betrayal."

Her bark-colored eyes widen. "You trust me?"

"Today? Barely." I tuck the juniper into my pocket. "But you're wrong about Veramis being more powerful than us. Together, we're ten times what she is."

Outside, a chorus of laughter floats from the town square. I pause at the shop door, Torren and Marlena staying close.

"Tell those in your army..." Her voice cracks. "Aim for their left chest and shoulder blades where a heart should be. The queen's magic is weakest there."

I nod and jut my chin toward the back of her shop. "Whatever you're keeping locked behind that door? Be careful with it." I suspect it's the result of a spell gone wrong. "If you need help, you know where I live."

The bell over the door jingles as we step onto the sidewalk.

A group of children rushes past, laughing and waving red and pink balloons.

So many mortals to save. I break into a run myself, worry snapping at my heels like an invisible Corgi.

And somewhere beyond our town, the frozen creek snaps under unseen weight.

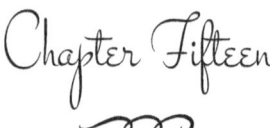

Chapter Fifteen

We've left Izzy and Flower running the shop, which might account for the long line we see when we return.

Marlena hustles to the back to grab our aprons. I focus on customers as Flower floats about, unable to do more than chat about the festivities. Izzy is frazzled, and I see her rubbing her temple. "Another migraine?" I ask as I hand Mrs. Winters her turnovers and a coffee.

"It's just a dull, throbbing ache," Izzy assures me.

Marlena passes out butterscotch candies to those waiting in line, thanking them for their patience. Torren grabs an order pad and goes down the line behind her, scribbling down requests. He returns and lines up the orders with military precision. I put him in charge of the register while Izzy and I stuff bags and fill cups with tea and coffee.

Two familiar figures squeeze through the open door. Hansel's crossbow barely clears the frame. Gretel's braids are threaded with fresh ivy.

"Have you had breakfast?" I ask.

Gretel crosses to a display and digs into a jar of chocolate-covered espresso beans. "These are all I need."

Hansel motions for Torren to follow him to the back room. Marlena is out of drops and follows to restock her basket. Izzy and Gretel wave me off so I can also join them. "We've reinforced the eastern wards," Hansel tells us. "I'm still concerned about that Witching Well, though."

While I gather an order of sugar cookies for one of our customers, Marlena hands him two steaming travel mugs. "Chai with extra cardamom. It's enchanted to shield you from Veramis' magic. One for you and one for your sister."

Cyn rushes in through the back door. "We forgot about McAllister Stern's orchards. Those would be a good place for Veramis to hide."

"Craggy bluffs are more her style," Marlena says. "I still think we should arm ourselves and search them."

Torren helps me with the cookies, taping the written order to the top of the box. "There are dozens of caves along the river. If she's planning to make a move during the festival, we don't have time to search them all."

"But we can check the path every hour to make sure none of her soldiers are headed our way," Hansel says. He sips his chai. "Gretel and I will start with that now."

I wait until they're gone before turning to Marlena. "They're going to the orchards first."

She fills a tray with fresh apple muffins. "I'd bet your prized candied violets on it."

Outside, the sky grows cloudy. I snap my fingers, and every light in the shop comes on, sending prismatic shards dancing across the jars and displays. I connect the chocolate fountain, and customers *ooh* and *ahh* over it. Torren hands the customer her box of cookies, and Marlena begins distributing more butterscotch drops. We put a drop of protective magic in each batch.

The day blurs into a constant stream of folks buying our goods. Mayor Jo stops by to tell us everything is going smoothly. He insists Torren go with him to check on the parade lineup.

When inventory gets low, I send a pale Izzy to the back to work on lollipops, hot cinnamons, and caramels.

Dr. Onley, from two blocks over, pushes up his reading glasses and peers into the nearly bare display case. "Those velvet creams I got here yesterday...do you have any more?"

"Behind the counter special," I whisper and wink, "reserved for our favorite customers." I knew he'd be back, and I had the foresight to save a dozen of the delicious vanilla confections for him. "These are sure to delight Lilibeth and win her heart."

"Thank you, dear," he says, blushing at the reference to his crush as he pays. "If they do, I'll owe you one."

He leaves, and Marlena's sudden stillness catches my eye. She's staring out the window, and so is Lady Wyndolynn. The sky is growing darker. Hansel and Gretel's distant figures hover in the town square near the Witching Well. My godmother's knuckles are white on a nearly empty jar of chocolate-covered espresso beans.

"What's wrong?" I ask, bumping her elbow gently with mine.

She sighs and glances back toward the display case. "Remember when a bad day here meant burnt marshmallows or a broken stove instead of a dark queen taking over the world?"

Before I can answer, the twins' magic ripples through the town, subtle but noticeable. Outside, the clouds threaten rain.

"Is Ms. Nyssa stirring up her rain curtains?"

Marlena shrugs. "Remind me why we didn't become accountants when we came to town?"

"Because you'd stab people with your letter opener, and I'd turn tax forms into lollipops."

Her laugh echoes through the shop. Flower appears and hiccups, a bubble emerging from her mouth. Izzy brings out a fresh batch of fudge. For this suspended moment, I can hope everything is going to be okay. We have a town to save, and I hope my candies and confections will help.

There's a knock at the back door. Izzy goes to answer it, while I wait on the next customer. Outside, a passing troupe of musicians plays a jaunty rendition of *Love Potion No. 9*.

Izzy returns with a beautiful bouquet of lilacs and ranun-culi in hand. "Flowers," she says with a smile. She holds up a pink paper note. "For me."

"Oooh," Flower says.

Marlena swipes the note, eyeing it suspiciously. "Who sent them?"

"I don't know." Izzy's smile grows. "It doesn't say, but Hansel knows that lilacs are my favorite."

"And so does your mother," I say, hating that her smile disappears. "I'm sorry, Iz, but we can't take chances. Those flowers stay outside until Hansel confirms he sent them."

She marches out.

By late afternoon, we're out of all baked goods and most of our candies. We have to close early, but I'm dead on my feet and am secretly relieved.

In the back, we clean trays and wash out jars. The bouquet is gone and Izzy's pout could curdled cream. She anxiously checks the front windows every few minutes for Hansel. The clouds still roil, but no rain falls.

The temperature in the shop drops and Torren appears at the worktable, holding a single black dahlia that drips what looks like liquid rubies. His grin could melt an entire iceberg. "For the woman who already owns every sweet thing in town," he says, holding out the flower to me.

Marlena's protective magic flares. My traitorous pulse gallops. The dahlia's petals curl into a shape disturbingly reminiscent of a crown.

Flower chooses that moment to swoop through the wall, wearing a tie-dyed skirt and sporting a pasta strainer as a helmet. "Behold!" she trumpets, waving a spatula. "The ghost of romance past, present, and... oh, hey, is that chocolate?"

Torren pulls back the dahlia. "Cupid's supposed to have arrows, not cookware."

She swirls around him, leaving frost patterns in her wake. "Mr. Tall-Dark-and-Immortal brought you murder flowers, Sera! That's practically a marriage proposal in vampyre circles!"

Torren's chuckle resonates in my bones, but I hide my hands behind my back. "I assure you no proposal is tucked amongst the petals. Merely an invitation to tonight's patrol. I'd prefer dinner and a casual stroll in the moonlight, but because of our current circumstances, this is the best I can offer for Valentine's Day."

Marlena slams a set of dirty trays onto the table. Izzy rolls her eyes. Flower throws spectral confetti. The dahlia whispers *mine* in a voice that curls around my ribs and tickles my heart.

Another pulse of Hansel and Gretel's magic flows through town.

"Flower, you and Izzy check on the twins, will you?" I say. "Make sure all is well?"

Izzy leaps for her jacket and is gone without waiting for the ghost.

Flower sticks out her tongue, not at her but at me. "You're no fun when Mr. Midnight Eyes is around." She drifts backward, eyeing the dahlia.

Torren snags a glass and fills it with water. He places the stem inside. "I must be going as well. I'm keeping an eye on the floats during the parade. Cynric's probably chewing through the clock tower by now, wondering where I am, but I'll see you later?"

We all glance at the dahlia. It doesn't drip rubies nor whisper to me. "I'd like that," I say.

I gather a few strawberry chews. "Take these to Cynric. Food always mollifies him."

His fingers brush mine as he accepts the bag. For half a heartbeat, the shop disappears, and all I see are his gorgeous eyes.

Marlena clears her throat. Torren smiles at me and leaves.

"Child." My godmother returns to washing trays. "When you play with danger—"

"He's the least dangerous thing on my plate at the moment." I fiddle with a bag of chocolate chips as I eye the flower. "And I just want to be normal sometimes. I'd like to enjoy Valentine's Day."

"He's a centuries-old predator." She sprays a tray. "You're being suckered by his charm."

Laughter filters in from outside. I go to the front windows, watching Torren glide past the revelers, heading toward City Hall, where the floats are lining up. "I know," I whisper.

Marlena sidles up to me, drying her hands on a towel. "Knowing's the easy part. Now convince your pulse."

The parade proceeds as planned. We watch from the sidewalk, keeping an eye out for trouble but seeing none. Izzy drifts in as the last float goes by. "The bouquet is from Hansel," she informs us before retrieving it.

We go inside, and I lock the door, putting the closed sign up. I'm relieved that the festival has so far been a success. Izzy carries in her bouquet, looking a bit wilted, and slaps a sleeve of roses onto the counter next to it. "Guess your boyfriend left these," she says to me.

The roses are flawless. Blood-red. Thornless. "He already gave me a dahlia." I point to the flower in the glass.

A rose petal detaches. It floats upward, rotating slowly until it presses itself to the ceiling. *MINE* appears in scrawled handwriting.

"He's rather possessive, isn't he?" Izzy says.

Marlena grabs the stack of clean trays. "I keep warning her to stay away from him."

All the roses unfurl with a wet *snick*. Thorns erupt along the stems. Marlena's clean trays hit the floor with a clatter, and Izzy jumps back with a yelp.

"Look out!" I lunge across the counter, but I'm too late.

Vines whip around Izzy's wrists, thorns drawing blood beads that float to feed the central bloom. It bursts wide, rows of jagged teeth glistening with saliva that sizzles when it hits the floor.

Marlena uses a broom handle to crack the plant's thickening stem. "Since when do roses have teeth?"

"Since Veramis took up landscaping."

Izzy kicks at a creeping tendril. Her sneaker smokes where acid eats through the rubber.

I scoop rock salt from its container. "Catch!" The pink granules arc through the air just as the central stalk bulges grotesquely, bursting into three snapping heads.

Izzy snags two pieces. "What do I do with it?"

"Throw it in their mouths!"

The roses shudder, sending out roots that tear through the sleeve as the salt foams into pink cement.

Izzy stumbles and screeches again. "What now?"

A thorny stem spears toward her throat. I grab the nearest thing I can reach—the chocolate fountain ladle—and smack the thing repeatedly. The plant screams in a chorus of Veramis's voice layered with Izzy's.

Marlena uses a tray to whack at the roots. It convulses, forming Queen Veramis's face. In her raspy snarl, it says, "*My darling Isadora... meddlesome confectioner... traitorous godmother...*"

Izzy's face turns red. "Talk to me in person, you coward!"

The table trembles as the creature swells, thorns punching holes through the ceiling. I duck a spray of acid, using a tray to deflect it.

Racing to the fountain, I dip the ladle in its still-warm chocolate and head back to the creature. I toss the chocolate in its face. The head lets out another cry before freezing mid-snap —teeth inches from Izzy's nose.

Panting, I press a hand to my heart and put an arm around Izzy's shoulder. "Sorry, Iz."

"I can't believe she'd do this to me," she says. "My own mother."

Marlena shoots me a glance that says, *classic Veramis.*

Outside, the festival music plays on.

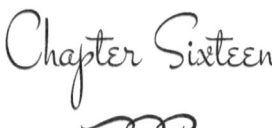

Chapter Sixteen

Even though Veramis attacked Izzy, nothing else happens. The evening's lantern lighting ceremony and the romantic gala dance at City Hall go on.

Torren, Cynric, Hansel, and Gretel continue their patrols and lookouts. Plenty of the Outcasts who got my message from Trinken join them to keep an eye on things.

We destroy the roses, and I even toss out the dahlia. I'm too gun shy about plants at the moment to feel safe with any around. Izzy, too, decides that her bouquet from Hansel will have to remain in my garden.

After a quick stroll through town to see the red and pink lanterns, I return to the shop. Candy is what I need to calm my nerves and keep my spirits up. Izzy has gone to bed after drinking a potion of a memory moss brew I found in an old recipe book. Marlena is out with the others, keeping her eye on things.

I'm elbow-deep in raspberry truffles when a familiar baritone cuts through the hum of my mixer. "Ambrosia."

My spine stiffens. I haven't heard that voice in months.

I whirl toward the front and take a few unsteady steps. The door was locked since we're closed, but there, framed by the heart-shaped wreaths and hovering lanterns outside the display windows, stand my parents.

Mother's silver-threaded gown glows faintly against the shop's walls while Father's ceremonial sword flashes under the lights.

"Your shop is lovely," the queen says.

My throat tightens. Five months since they banned me from my realm. Five months since I last saw the midnight-blue banners of Ever After's royal chambers. Yet here they stand between the fountain and the display case, looking profoundly out of place.

Father gives a curt nod. "We received your warning about Veramis."

"I, uh...didn't expect you to come in person," I manage, wiping my hands on my apron. "Last we spoke, you exiled me. Made me an Outcast."

Mother flinches. Good.

Her hands grip the folds of her gown. "We've learned that Veramis' treachery may have been involved in what happened that day."

"We were wrong." Father has always been the more forthright about his mistakes. Mother, not so much. "Veramis has corrupted many things, Ambrosia. I—*we*—want to set things right."

I step closer. Their crowns shimmer with old magic that makes me long for them even more. Not the rulers of Ever After, but the mother and father who once nurtured and loved me more than anything. "You believe me now? About the fact that I'm innocent of murder?"

"We believe," Mother says quietly. "About that and how

Veramis' has a master plan to use you and Izzy to get what she's always wanted."

Footsteps on the stairs make me turn. Izzy, all wild hair and trembling hands, calls my name as she nearly tumbles down the last few steps. "Sera, the memory moss worked. I know what happened that day."

She pulls up short at the sight of my parents. Dips a curtsy. "Your Majesties," she breathes. "What a...surprise!"

"Princess Isadora." Mother offers a gracious, royal smile. "It is good to see you."

Izzy's eyes dart to me. "My mother planted false evidence against Ambrosia. Made everyone think she killed me, but she didn't." She rubs her temples and squints. "Obviously. But... there was this rose bush. Black thorns. She told me it was a birthday surprise for Ambrosia." She slaps a hand over her lips. "Oh, lemon tarts. I mean, Seraphina."

"It's okay, Iz," I say, rushing to her. "They know. " To them, I explain, "Memory suppression. A curse. We've all been tampered with, but for her, it's worse."

Mother clicks her tongue. Father shakes his head. "Forbidden magic," he says.

My chest aches. "What else did you remember?" I ask Izzy.

"Everything, but you don't want to hear it."

The curse is broken. She remembers.

Mother steps forward, skirts shushing. "We'll convene the High Council. With Isadora's testimony, we'll clear your name, Ambrosia."

"They'll demand proof," Father interrupts. "Veramis owns half the arbiters."

"Then we'll replace them!" My voice rises. "She's a traitor to the realm. When do we stop playing her game?"

Izzy's hand finds mine, no longer trembling but steady. "When we cheat better."

A gnome messenger barrels in, hat askew and beard in knots. "Hansel sent me. The Queen's soldiers, Princess! At the Witching Well! They're—"

He realizes the King and Queen of Ever After are present and gulps, dropping to one knee with a bent head. "Begging your pardons, but"—he jumps up—"it's all hands on deck!"

Mother's crown flares brighter. "Leon?"

Father draws his sword. It gleams. "Ambrosia, have Trinken escort you and Isadora back to Ever After."

Outside, screams rip through the air. Onyx flares to life, and I grab handfuls of candies. "We stay. This is our home to protect."

For a heartbeat, no one moves. Then Mother smiles—the real one that crinkles her eyes. "To arms, then. But afterward," —she eyes my fountain—"we're discussing proper throne room decor."

Hansel and Gretel arrive, sending the gnome back to the fight. Both are shocked to see my parents and while they acknowledge the pair with honor, they buzz with impatience. "Veramis," Hansel starts, and Mother lifts a hand.

"We know," she says.

"It started with roses." Izzy's eyes are unfocused. Her typical softness is replaced by something rigid—betrayal. Her pupils dilate, swallowing the obsidian sparkle I'm used to as more memories flood back. "They weren't normal. Curled too tight, like fists. Mother said we had to make an offering to Ever After's gardens for Ambrosia. That she would use the petals for candies."

Queen Veramis planted poisoned roses in the royal gardens. I should be scandalized, but I'm not in the least surprised.

Izzy presses a thumbnail into her palm. "I knelt to smell them. Thorns snagged my sleeve. Felt like spider legs dragging me closer."

A drop of blood wells on her skin, sudden and garish. Hansel shifts forward, his instincts overriding decorum to stop her from harming herself.

Gretel places a hand on his chest and shakes her head. "Let her speak."

"Everything went hot," Izzy whispers. "My pulse became war drums. Your faces were wrong. Twisted."

"And we found you wandering in the forest," Gretel says.

"*Found* me?" Izzy's voice cracks. "I hunted you. The spell tasted smoky and sour. I remember swinging the fireplace poker, screaming things about traitors..." She looks at me properly for the first time.

Hansel's s gaze stays locked on her bleeding palm. "You kept shouting about stolen thrones. We thought..."

"That I was starting a coup?" Izzy finishes.

The memories now are mine, too. I nod. "We all did."

A siren erupts in the streets. The King glances out the windows. "Where was Veramis during this?"

"Watching." Izzy spits the word. "From her enchanted mirror. When I woke up covered in ashes and blood, she told me how tragically I'd 'fallen under Ambrosia's influence.' How she'd contained me to protect my future." Her broken laugh shreds my heart. "She fed me a sleeping potion, and the next thing I knew, I was in this realm with my spirit tied to that Cambria witch who forced me to do her bidding."

Queen Lethia sucks in a breath, anger staining her cheeks. "That venomous crone staged her own daughter's death and then sold her to a witch?"

"To frame our daughter," Father growls. "To overthrow our peaceful kingdom."

Izzy slumps against the display case. "Every time I tried to remember, the rage came back. So I stopped trying. I did what Cambria wanted." Her tearful eyes flick up at me. "I'm so sorry."

I pull her into a hug. "You have nothing to be sorry for."

Her smile's a fragile thing as we break apart. "You're still my best friend after all of this?"

I squeeze her hands. "Suck it up, buttercup. You can't get rid of me that easily."

More screams. The ground trembles. Our soldier guests have arrived.

Hansel unsheathes Dradus. "Time to stop the evil queen."

Mother clasps Izzy's shoulders. "All will be sorted once this is over."

Fresh fear slams into me as we step out onto the sidewalk. "You need to go," I say to my parents. "Return to Ever After."

Mother shakes her head. "We didn't come here to turn around and hide behind our daughter."

Mayor Jo, Cynric, and Torren charge toward us. The mayor nods to my parents as I share introductions. "Nice to meet you. You have an amazing daughter. Try not to die. It plays havoc with the property values."

King Leon's chuckle rumbles as deep as thunder. "We'll endeavor to postpone our deaths until we are back home."

I hand out bags of candies with instructions, and Gretel informs them about the iron repelling the shadow ghouls but admits she isn't sure if it will destroy them. Marlena appears, and Izzy tells her of her memory recall.

"You've prepared well," Mother says to me while they discuss the soldiers' weak spots near where a heart should be.

"Had to." I press a vial of rainbow sprinkles into her palm. "When you're the exiled princess in a realm filled with humans, you have to get creative."

A chorus of snarls pierces the night. Izzy's fingers dig into my arm. "They're hunting us."

Father's cloak billows as he strides forward. "Then we redirect the hunt."

We're an odd cluster of misfits. Torren, Hansel, Gretel, Marlena, Cynric, Mayor Jo, Izzy, and I line up on either side of the King and Queen. Ms. Nyssa appears, hurrying down the street with bottles of potions in hand. Mr. Thornwick approaches with a pitchfork. I welcome them both.

"Now," I say as the ground continues to tremble and the snarls echo through the air. "We're a force to be reckoned with."

Chapter Seventeen

People scream, running past us. Onyx burns on my collarbone.

We speed down Main Street, my boots sliding on slick cobblestones—some poor soul dropped their red velvet cupcakes—and suddenly, I'm drowning in a nightmare version of our festival.

The streets are a chaotic mess of shattered Valentine displays, trampled flowers, and busted candy heart boxes. We fight our way through the fleeing crowd. Above us, the paper hearts and lanterns strung between lampposts ignite one by one, burning ashes falling like snow. The angry clouds overhead seem far too low as they electrify the night air and pitch us into an unnatural, murky darkness.

Torren grabs my elbow, yanking me behind Hansel's bulk as three shadow ghouls crash through the teashop's front windows. The soldiers move all wrong, their joints bending sideways and their shadows stretching longer than their bodies. Glass crunches under their stone feet.

One of Gretel's arrows whizzes past a group of teens huddling near the dentist's office. It embeds itself in the eye socket of one of the monsters. "Get out of here!" she calls to the kids, nocking another arrow. "Hansel! Watch your six!"

He spins. "Noted!" While the teens run, she takes down the other two, and he leaps in front of my mother as he uses his crossbow to knock a shadow ghoul sneaking up behind us to the ground.

My father vaults forward, piercing the thing's clay armor with his enchanted sword. It disintegrates. My mother gives him a grateful smile.

Trinken and his wife join us, a band of armed faeries with them. When they see my parents, there is much confusion as to whether they should bow, kneel, or give a report. All three happen simultaneously, and the King holds up his sword to silence everyone.

Mother reaches out to lift people from their knees. "No time for formalities," she tells them. "We need to shield the town and protect the humans."

"Goblins to the northern flank," Torren orders.

Hansel booms, "Faeries, to the east!"

My magic prickles under my skin. "If you encounter soldiers, aim for their left shoulder blades," I call to all of them, and Ms. Nyssa gives me a nod.

Mother gathers us in a semi-circle. "We need to construct a shield. Ambrosia and I will take the structural support. Night-walker, you're on princess duty." She grabs Torren's arm. "You protect her with your life, undead as it may be."

"Yes, Your Majesty," he says, giving me a wink.

As Cynric and Mayor Jo herd people behind us, Mother orders Marlena and Izzy into place to anchor our spell, then instructs me to use my butterscotch and caramel candies to form a barrier.

When the next trio of soldiers rushes us, Ms. Nyssa pours

her potions on the street in a fat line in front of the growing shield. The cobblestones sizzle and smoke, and when the soldiers step on the acid, it eats their legs up to their knees. They drop to the ground, and Hansel and Mr. Thornwick make quick work of them.

My shield begins to rise in a golden, gooey screen. "Thicker on the left!" Marlena barks. She has Gunther in one hand and a witchlight glowing in the other.

Torren's fangs glint as he bites his wrist, dark master vampyre blood arcing through the air to mix with my enchanted candy. The barrier ripples crimson where it catches the light, gaining an extra layer of resilience.

When I flinch at the metallic tang now woven into my confection, he grins. "Blood's just another sweetener, Princess."

We almost have the dome sealed when a high-pitched wail slices through the battle din. Through the honey and blood-tinged barrier, I spot Maude scrambling over a toppled Cupid statue. "Seraphina," she shrieks. "Help!"

"Stay behind the barrier," Father orders.

Maude clutches a bleeding shoulder and can't seem to gain her feet. "*Help*," she cries again.

"I'll take care of her," Torren says. "You stay here."

But I'm already running, tossing a trail of jawbreakers at a group of soldiers bearing down on her. When they step on the round candies, they lose their balance and go down, arms cartwheeling.

"Seraphina! Wait!" Torren's footsteps echo behind mine as I reach Maude.

Izzy sprints to me. "Greenhouse," she gasps, shoving my mother's brooch into my hand. Its prongs bite my palm. "My connection to Mother just showed me she's there."

"Get back inside the barrier," my mother commands in her royal voice. The order of rule vibrates my very bones.

Marlena lobs a cinnamon and clove grenade that whizzed by over our heads. It explodes against a charging soldier's chest, and hard clay chunks rain down on us. "I've got the dentist," she says, practically lifting Maude from off the ground and carting her to the barrier.

The brooch burns cold in my hand. I run for the greenhouse. Izzy and Torren keep pace, and I'm amazed that the vamprye doesn't complain.

I spot poisoned chrysanthemums outside the tea shop. Or what's left of it—the entire storefront's encased now in deadly vines. Inside, teacups rattle on their saucers, overflowing with viscous purple liquid. The scent of rotting violets engulfs us.

Mr. Thornwick is breathing heavily as he catches up to us. "That woman is at my place again?"

"I'm afraid so," I tell him.

"Then I'm coming with you."

The Faerie Bloom sign comes into view as we duck around more fleeing pedestrians. The usual cheery greenhouse panes glow poisonous green, and tendrils of mist coil under the doors. Izzy gags at the smell of overcooked fertilizer.

"Stay behind me," Torren orders, though we both ignore him. Through the warped glass, I glimpse movement—not plants, but shapes that might have been human once, now tangled in choking vines.

Izzy's fist hovers over the door handle. "We can do this, right, Sera?"

I squeeze her arm. "We can and we will."

When the door creaks open, the humidity hits us, my hair drooping under the moisture. Rows of potted plants hang limp in their planters, petals edged with fungus. Deeper in the greenhouse, something heavy drags across the concrete floor.

Torren inhales sharply. "Everything is laced with evil."

The door slams shut behind us, and we all jump. Mr. Thornwick thumps his pitchfork on the floor. "I'm not going down without a fight!" he yells into the heavy air.

Queen Veramis appears in the center of the rows. She caresses an orchid's throat, her emerald gown shimmering with the same toxic green as the stones in her crown. As we watch, she breathes across the plant's gaping maw—a lover's whisper that makes its tendrils double in size.

The orchid detaches from its stem with a wet pop. Dozens more blooms, including dahlias and lilies follow, forming a floating garden of death that hovers around us.

The queen murmurs under her breath and the entire collection of plants seems to lean toward her like subjects bowing.

Izzy's hand finds mine, ice-cold. "She's weaponizing the ecosystem."

"Darling," Veramis says without looking at her, "you brought me exactly what I asked for."

"Mother, stop this. The festival—"

"Will make an excellent fertilizer base." A woman cries for help beyond the windows, and a nearby rosebush erupts in blossoms the color of infected wounds. "Observe, Isadora. This cultivar reacts splendidly to agony."

Torren steps forward, sword in hand. "Your master plan has failed. I suggest you surrender."

A vine cracks next to his ear—a warning. The queen smiles. "You'll speak when I tell you to, leech."

My magic snaps out of me, causing the overhead lights to shatter. Veramis tilts her head as fractured pieces of glass catch in the silver pins holding her crown in place. "Oh, Ambrosia. Still playing the disgraced heroine of your sad little faerytale."

Izzy makes a choking sound. Veramis flicks her gaze to her. "Come here, Isadora. Take your rightful place beside me."

Izzy glares. "You lied. You betrayed us all. You're a traitor to the realm."

Thorny vines from a rosebush creep toward Izzy's ankles as the floating blooms hover closer to her face. She bats at them, but I recognize this classic distraction play—evil monologue while the real attack uncoils at our feet.

I'm not up for her excuses or reasons for her actions. I hurl a gumdrop. It smacks her in her smug face, shocking her. I infuse my voice with every bit of royal blood inside me. "Leave Izzy alone."

Veramis snarls. Izzy yelps as thorns tear through her skirt and bite into her leg. Torren lunges to slice the vines, but a hanging basket spits acid on him. He spins to strike it instead. Mr. Thornwick raises his pitchfork and sends it sailing through the air, stabbing the rosebush.

The queen's laughter twines through the chaos, and a Venus flytrap the size of a bulldog snaps at my head. "You can't hurt me, you stupid candy shop witch," she sneers.

Torren shoves me aside, and I stumble behind a wheelbarrow. Across the way, a wall of kudzu springs to life, cutting him off from me and Izzy.

I lob gummy bears at the queen. They swell into snarling guardians. "Take care of Izzy," I order the master vampyre. "I've got the wicked witch."

He hesitates, sword halfway through the tangle of kudzu. His eyes meet mine, and I see the conflict in his dark irises. "You're certain?"

A rose thorn grazes my cheek. I swipe at it, and it snags the skin of my arm. "Yes. Do it!"

He disappears in a blur of sword strikes. I knot licorice whips to form a net to cover the attacking rosebush. The whips entangle in the bush's stems, and it tries to pitch them off.

The queen tuts, shredding my gummy defenders with claw-tipped fingers. With a flick of her wrist, she sends the pitchfork sailing back to the greenhouse owner. Mr. Thornwick ducks behind a pile of topsoil bags as the tines stab into the floor where he previously stood.

The ground heaves and breaks open. What emerges isn't a plant. Not an animal, either. Just a mass of twitching chlorophyll and teeth. I backpedal, rummaging through my pockets. Rock candy for spears? Caramel to form a suppression blanket? Oh, heck, birthday cake sprinkles to form grenades?

Izzy shouts my name. "Sera!"

The sprinkles will have to do.

They explode like fireworks, coating the monstrosity in rainbow dust that sizzles where it lands. The thing shrieks, causing me to cover my ears. My nostrils burn from the acrid smoke.

Queen Veramis drifts through the carnage, her gown whispering against the cracked floor. "Adorable theatrics." She flicks her other wrist. The creature's wounds knit together. It grows a set of mandibles. "But Princess," she croons, and I'm unsure whether she means me or Izzy until she says, "why bring strays to our family reunion?"

"You lost the right to call me family," Izzy says with no small amount of sadness, "when you framed Ambrosia for my murder."

Torren breaks free of the kudzu.

"Grab her," I call to him. "That's an order from your future queen!"

His laughter is easy and calm as he uses his vampyre speed to reach Izzy's side. "Is that a marriage proposal, Seraphina? And here I thought you weren't sweet on me."

Veramis clicks her tongue. "How predictable." She blows a kiss toward the roof.

The glass ceiling shatters. A dozen mutated honeysuckles pour through, vines seeking us out. One catches Torren across the cheekbone as he shields Izzy. Another wraps around my waist. I lob a gumball into my mouth and bite down hard.

I chew fast, then smear the sticky mass onto the vine. It recoils from my magic, giving me a few seconds to follow the gum plaster with a smear of fireball cinnamon discs. That does the trick, the vine retreating to the ceiling.

I pant and try to take Veramis' focus off Izzy. "You need my royal blood to thwart my parents and take over Ever After." I step from my hiding place. "Well, here I am."

Torren's voice cuts through the air. "Seraphina! What are you doing?"

Veramis adjusts her crown. I feel a surge in the ley lines far underneath this place. No wonder she chose the greenhouse to form her wicked plan. "Let's discuss terms."

I stride past Torren and Izzy. "Terms require mutual interests."

"Do they?" She strolls past a wilting hydrangea that shivers. The flower blooms bob around me. "Your little candy shop could remain untouched. Your friends might even survive the night." Her eyes gleam. "All you have to do is bleed for me."

Ice tightens my throat. "That's not how this agreement is going to go. I have the upper hand here. You may be *a* queen, but you will never be The Queen, the ruler of the entire realm.

Only the high royal line that belongs to my family can hold that crown."

Veramis sucks on a tooth. "But I've rewritten the story, Ambrosia. Your faerytale has been erased."

I shatter seed packets with a licorice whip, unleash fertilizer clouds with candy daggers, and toss a lemon drop into the flytrap's maw, commanding it to eat the deadly floating dahlias, lilies, and all.

Torren grabs Izzy around the waist and dashes for the exit.

Veramis materializes inches from my face. "Persistent *pest*," she spits.

Onyx is about to burst into gargoyle form. I can't have that —it will destroy the greenhouse entirely. I grip my mother's brooch as I telepathically command my protector not to morph. "You have no idea."

I strike first.

Her shadow tendrils meet my exploding candies in a shower of sparks. The force knocks us apart. I skid across bags of peat moss, she lands gracefully atop a propagating table.

Between us, the greenhouse seems to breathe a death rattle. Glass panes groan in their frames. Support beams creak. Somewhere, a faucet explodes, spraying water that bubbles where it touches dark magic residue.

Veramis blows across her fingertips—darkness coalescing into a swirling portal. She's getting away!

I lunge, catching her in an awkward embrace and taking her down. We land in the rosebush, and she shrieks as the thorns impale her.

Her next gasp lingers in the air for a heartbeat. I toss a lemon drop into her mouth. "I command you to return to Ever After, where you'll be punished for your treason." Her skin cracks, and her body ripples. I jump away as she fades into a shadow and disappears completely.

Torren crashes through the debris. "Sera—"

"Check the perimeter." I push him off me. "She might've left surprises."

He hesitates, midnight eyes scanning me from head to toe. "You're injured."

"I'm fine." I nod toward Mr. Thornwick, who is cowering behind the bags. "Get him out of here. Now."

As he does my bidding, I sag against the potting station. Across the decimated garden center, Mayor Jo, Hansel, Gretel, and my parents appear. "Where is she?" Mother asks.

"Back in Ever After. I hope you have guards waiting for her."

Father gives a brusque nod. "The entire kingdom is waiting to impart justice on her."

"I've never been so happy with your lemon drops," Torren says, helping Mr. Thornwick to his feet. "Or your gumballs, licorice, and gummy bears."

He comes to me and brushes at a scratch on my face. "Now, about that future queen comment."

I hide my smile and wave him off. "Tomorrow, Torren. We'll discuss it tomorrow."

Chapter Eighteen

I find the town square swimming in beautiful moonlight and relieved citizens. The clouds are gone, everyone's alive, and while there's plenty of cleanup to do and questions to answer, all the shadow ghouls have disappeared.

Marlena perches on the Witching Well's rim, dabbing at Izzy's forehead with a rag.

Izzy waves weakly, and I wave back. "Is she gone for good?" my friend asks, and I swear her tone holds both hope and grief.

Torren helps me over a spilled drink. "She's gone," I say, squeezing her shoulder. "I'm sorry for what she did to you."

Ms. Nyssa tosses me a vial of thick pink liquid. "Drink. Unless you enjoy looking like chewed bubblegum."

I'm wary of anything she offers, but we seem to have come to a truce and she wouldn't dare harm me after I just saved the town. Would she? I down the concoction and find it isn't as bad as anticipated. A warmth spreads through my tired limbs and I feel moderately better.

Could still use some chocolate, though.

The crowd parts as Mayor Jo leads me and Torren to City

Hall's steps. Folks gather to hear what we're going to say. At least a hundred expectant faces tilt up, some sporting dirt smears, grass stains, and scratches. At the rear, Outcasts add their numbers to the throng.

"The town is safe," I begin. "The mastermind behind this is no longer a threat." Cheers erupt, and people clap.

"Hansel?" Mayor Jo gestures for him to join us. "What's your report?"

The warrior clears his throat as he stops next to me. "The army is dust. The good kind. Fertilizer-grade."

Gretel nods and says, "We're calling it Operation Compost."

Chuckles roll through the square, gaining momentum. The trio of teens from earlier start a conga line past the Witching Well. Flower jumps up and down, even though she's floating several feet off the ground, clapping her hands. "Is the festival over?" she asks.

"Not yet," I murmur, and when Mayor Jo gives me a questioning look, I raise my voice to the crowd, "I know we've all been through a lot tonight, and many of you have questions. Let's tackle all of that tomorrow, okay? For now, hug your loved ones and come by my shop for some Valentine's punch and whatever we have left for treats. It's on the house!"

Another cheer goes up, and I move as quickly as my stiff body allows, with the others falling into step with me.

Izzy limps over, allowing Marlena to help her. "You did it, Sera."

"*We* did it." I squeeze her hand, feeling the truth in my sticky hair, my parents' quiet laughter behind me, and the brooch humming in my pocket. The street lamps come on, and The Candy Cauldron's windows show Lady Wyndolynn watching us.

When we get inside, my mother pulls me into a hug. "Come here, daughter."

For a heartbeat, I'm six years old again, hiding in her skirts during summer storms. Then she sets me back a few steps. "Next time? Call us sooner."

"I didn't think you'd come."

She caresses my injured cheek. "We deserve that, but never doubt our love for you again."

The teens from the conga line march past carrying a banner. *Candy Queen* is painted in neon across the front. They hoot and give me a thumbs-up through the window.

"Subtle," Izzy deadpans.

"If they only knew the truth," Marlena says.

Cyn rounds up what he can find for treats and begins handing them out to those gathering outside. "It's a victory party!"

Marlena and Izzy throw together the ingredients for punch. I turn on the chocolate fountain. Torren makes tea and brings me a cup.

Father winks, offering me a piece of pound cake dipped in the melted chocolate. I don't ask where he found the cake. "I'm awarding Hansel and Gretel silver hearts for their bravery and courage," he tells me. "Looks like I must award the same to you, your vampyre, and the others."

"Don't forget Mr. Thornwick and Ms. Nyssa," I say, "and, honestly, I don't need one."

"How about we discuss it later?" Mother suggests.

It's long past midnight when the final revelers depart, the shop utterly devoid of food and drink. Even the chocolate fountain is empty.

I want to climb into bed and sleep for a week, but the best

time to clear the streets and wipe human memories of this tragic event is now.

I wait until the others are settled before I grab Torren's hand. "Come with me."

"A moonlit stroll? You look positively exhausted, fair princess. How about I tuck you in bed and tell you a story?"

I can't tell if he's serious or if this is innuendo. "There's still work to be done. The humans must forget any of this happened."

He waves me up the stairs to the second floor. "I will handle that on my own."

"But the cleanup—"

"Will be taken care of." He winks. "Goodnight, my future queen."

With that, he disappears.

Chapter Nineteen

Sunday, we're closed. Izzy and I sleep late and wake to find a note from Marlena telling us to come to the church.

The streets are mostly clean. Dozens of Cyn's parishioners, Torren's vampyres, and a few city workers are boarding up the windows of the tea shop, sweeping up debris in the town center, and fixing the floor of the greenhouse. We find Marlena, Mayor Joe, Hansel, and Gretel at the church, handing out coffee and breakfast goods. Cyn is directing litter pickup and the filling of potholes in the sidewalks and streets.

Amid the supernaturals, humans discuss the 'storm' that came through, wrecking the end of the festival. Torren is not in sight, and although he needs very little sleep, I imagine he is resting after a long night of replacing people's memories of Veramis and her shadow ghouls with images of the phantom storm.

Hansel breaks away from his duties to hand Izzy a large coffee and a pastry. He leans in toward me, offering the same. "These aren't as good as yours, but we wanted to give you the day off."

Izzy hugs him and accepts the breakfast. "Tell us how we can help."

Gretel gestures for us to join her behind the buffet table. "We have a lot of mouths to feed."

Marlena stops me before I can follow Izzy. "You and I have work to do at the Witching Well."

My apple strudel pastry is pretty good, and it is with some surprise that I discover Maude is the baker. She catches up to us right before we reach the Well. "I see you have one of my masterpieces. Does it have enough sugar for you, Seraphina?"

I laugh. "The perfect amount. I didn't realize you had such skills."

She puts a finger to her lips. "Our little secret, okay? I can't have my outstanding reputation ruined by a Danish."

I give her a solemn promise that I won't share her secret, but she still puts me on the spot. "I've scheduled you for your yearly exam on Tuesday at six p.m.," she says. "I don't usually stay open in the evenings, but I know you work all day. For you, I'll make an exception."

How can I say no? It will be a quick appointment since my magic keeps my teeth in perfect condition. "I appreciate the consideration."

She leaves to help the group working on the tea shop, putting her arm around the owner as Marlena and I turn back to the Well. A huge chunk is missing from the lip, and the waters are bubbling in a sickly manner.

"That can't be good," I say, finishing my coffee.

Marlena studies the water. "I fear we're going to have to close down the Well for now until I can figure out what's causing it to brew like this."

I peer into the water, which reflects my image and the blue sky above. "It reminds me of a cauldron," I say.

"Me, too, and not in a good way. Did Veramis do something to it?"

I squint at the spot where the chunk is missing from the lip. It resembles an open mouth. "Possibly. If she did, the Well could spell trouble. We should ask the mayor to close it down for now. We'll need to analyze it and determine if it could harm anyone. I've never dealt with a bespelled wishing well, have you?"

A shake of her head. "Research is called for."

Hansel strides across the square. His forehead has a pensive crease. "Could I borrow you for a minute, Princess?"

"Of course," I say. "Is something wrong?"

He fiddles with the buttons of his jacket. "I am in need of your counsel. Gretel thinks I'm overstepping, but after last night, there's something I must do."

Marlena quirks a brow but makes excuses about finding Major Jo. A city worker walks by with yellow tape, and I instruct him to rope off the Well for now.

I guide Hansel a few feet away and lower my voice. "Does this have to do with Isadora?"

He nods. "She's remembering more about her life in Ever After. About...us."

A group of young children run past, playing tag and laughing. With their mothers trailing after them, the group heads for the park. I'm relieved it's a safe place again. "That's a good thing. Why do you look so sour?"

"She doesn't feel worthy of me after what her mother has done. And with Veramis out of the picture, the Black Heart Court is leaderless. Izzy must step into her role as the next queen, yet she refuses to entertain the idea. Darkness has crushed her spirit. How do I help her get it back?"

If only a dose of sugar would cure her. "I'm afraid it's not a simple fix. She has a lot of healing to do after being betrayed by her mother. And no one can force her to step into the role of queen." But he's right. Our friend will soon have to make a decision regarding her future. Her family's throne cannot go empty for long. "The best thing you can do is be a supportive friend."

He digs a toe into the cobblestones and gives a chuckle. "I wish to be more than that."

Color me shocked. *Not.* "Let's take a walk. I have an idea."

The bell above Spell Bound Books announces our arrival. "Not this place again," he mutters. "It smells like my grandmother's attic after a rainstorm."

A thick book on the nearest shelf flutters its pages at me in greeting. "Ah yes," I sniff the air, catching the old parchment and ink aroma. "Eau de forgotten knowledge and bottled nostalgia."

A quill scratches autonomously behind the counter. The shop owner is nowhere in sight.

Hansel pauses before a rotating display of pop-up books. His calloused finger hovers over a dancing pastry chef illustrated in spun sugar. "Hey, this looks a lot like you."

I notice the resemblance. One of these days, I need to investigate the magic of this place. "Yes, well, we need something unique for Isadora. Something magical."

"Welcome, fair readers!" We jump as the shop's proprietress materializes from a curtain of hanging bookmarks. Cossette Crimson, owner and bibliophile, adjusts her pince-nez glasses, the chains swinging next to her cheeks. "Princess. Guard Captain. Seeking solace in stories or solutions in sonnets?"

Hansel blinks at her as he squares his shoulders. "Our mutual friend requires a bit of whimsy. She's had a rough time lately."

Cossette places a finger to her chin, her gaze focusing on the air above our heads for a moment as she thinks. She snaps her fingers. "I've got just the thing."

The shop cat eyes us with speculation as we pass its perch on top of a collection of cozy mysteries. Cossette leads us to the back, where she pulls down a book on fireflies from the top shelf. When she opens it, it morphs into a pop-up book, tiny fireflies seeming to come to life and emerge from miniature flowers. She turns the page, and a small dragon alights from a cave where a crowned woman pets it. Each section contains a faerytale story enacted by enchanted creatures. The final one is of a princess accepting a crown of hearts and sitting on a throne. The paper model resembles Izzy.

Cossette's eyes are lit with mischief. "What do you think? Will this make her heart light once more?"

Hansel gives me a weighted look. "Is it perhaps prophetic?"

Cossette winks. "Who is to say, guard captain? Each of us creates our own future, do we not, in every moment, every breath."

"We'll take it," I tell her.

Later that evening when I walk out back, the garden air is alive with magic that makes my pulse skip. Hansel is reading to Izzy upstairs, his baritone voice a distance rumble. Marlena and Gretel are at the church with Cynric and Mayor Jo. Flower is off doing Flower things.

Between ivy-laced trellises, lighted gourds shaped like hearts hover at cheeky angles, their rays catching on the crystal goblets set atop my wrought-iron bistro table. Torren centered it in the garden, causing the herbs and flowers to awaken and grow as if it were the height of summer. Even the air temperature is warm.

He hovers over the table, arranging the silverware. Next to

it is a serving tray, its top filled with covered platters. "You received my message."

My voice comes out steadier than my traitorous heartbeat. I lean against the doorframe. "And you redecorated."

He doesn't turn, though I see the corner of his mouth quirk. "We have not had a chance to celebrate Valentine's Day." His pause feels deliberate, almost anticipatory. "I hoped you might find your garden a place to relax."

He pulls out a chair upholstered in moss-green velvet—an invitation. The scent of roasted garlic and thyme dancing with something darker and richer reaches my nose. My stomach betrays me with an audible murmur.

"Blood orange risotto," he says, gesturing to the steaming bowl that appears as I sit. "With porcini mushrooms foraged from the forest."

I trace the gilded rim of the plate. "Should I ask whose blood oranges you used?"

His teeth flash white in the heart-shaped spotlight glowing on us. "Only the finest in these parts, I assure you, and the chef happens to be at your service." He bows.

I blink. "You made dinner?"

A simple nod as he sits and pours wine for each of us. "I'm not without talents."

The first bite dissolves on my tongue, a creamy Arborio rice bursting with tangy sweetness. A moan escapes before I can stifle it.

At the sound, he stills, gaze landing on my lips. He leans back, shadows pooling in the hollow of his throat. "You like it?"

I swallow another bite, my lids fluttering in heavenly bliss. "I've never tasted anything so good."

The next few minutes pass in a blur of wine and delicious

courses. I'm stuffed by the time he pours coffee and serves dessert.

"I heard your parents have lifted your ban."

It's said off-handedly, yet I note the underlying question: will I be returning to Ever After?

I sip my coffee and avoid his eyes. "You've been gossiping with Lady Wyndolynn again."

"Your feline confidant merely expressed concerns over your future. She rather likes it here. I'm hoping you feel the same."

I flick my dessert spoon his direction. "While I must admit that it feels nice to no longer be an Outcast and to have the charges against me lifted, I have come to think of this place as home. I mean, who would give up working twelve hours a day with no holidays or weekends off and a near-constant assortment of mysteries to solve and evil-doers to stop?"

His laughter is sweeter than the honey drizzled on our shared fig tart. "You are something, Princess."

We discuss the Witching Well's issue and the upcoming spring celebration next month. March is the equinox and Easter, or Ostara as some celebrate it. There will be candy eggs and chocolate rabbits to make, spring vegetables to harvest, Simnel cakes to decorate, and hot cross buns to add spices to. We move to the swing under the willow tree and stay there until the constellations shift position, and the third button of his shirt comes undone with my fingers involvement. My cheeks ache from smiling and my cheeks are flushed.

When he reaches to brush a crumb from my lip, his thumb lingers. The garden holds its breath. "Seraphina." My name sounds different coming from his mouth—an enchantment.

The world narrows to the heat of his palm as it cradles my jaw, to the dangerous curve of his lower lip. Somewhere beyond the garden walls, a nightingale trills.

Our first kiss tastes of danger and inevitability.

Afterward, as we stack dishes in the sink, my thoughts bubble like those in the Well. This man could unravel all of my carefully constructed defenses.

He washes, and I dry. He catches me staring as a single soap droplet glides down his wrist. "Regrets, future queen?"

I press a thumb to the corner of his mouth, where his lips so often twitch in his version of a smile. "Not yet, vampyre."

But as I say goodbye to him and lock up an hour later, the garden and my body still vibrate with his magic. I trace my bottom lip, buzzing from his kisses, and wonder what ingredients make a love potion strong enough to survive immortality.

Moonlight coats the cobblestones outside as I stare out at the town. Lady Wyndolynn's tail flicks against my ankle. *You're humming*, she accuses, peering up with slit-pupiled disapproval.

"Am not."

She stalks toward the supply closet. Upstairs, I hear the gentle rumble of Hansel's voice and Izzy's lighthearted laughter. I'm not the only one enjoying a belated Valentine's Day.

That's when I smell it—dead flowers.

In the distance, magic pulses and warps the air. The door handle frosts under my palm. Beyond the threshold, Enchanted Haven sleeps...except for the Witching Well.

I hurry to it, feeling its call. A plea, really.

For help.

The yellow tape flaps in an invisible breeze. The Well's water swirls ink-black.

"Oh, crumbs."

Tourist coins glint beneath the murky surface, but it's an unusual addition that chills me—a single obsidian hairpin floating on the water and spinning like a compass needle.

Lady Wyndolynn materializes on the lip of the Well. She hisses at the hairpin.

It leaps from the water, embedding itself in the plank overhead. A scrap of parchment uncurls from its grip:

Dearest Candy Witch,

How quaint, your little shop. Let's discuss recipes.

-Your secret admirer

Across the square, the glow from Alchemy Elixirs darkens abruptly, and every window slams shut.

Somewhere in the distance, Flower screams.

___

I hope you enjoyed Gum & Ghouls! What mystery awaits Seraphina and her friends next? Find out in Sweets & Spirits, releasing in 2026.

If you haven't read the whole series yet, check out Tricks & Treats, Witchy Candy Shop Series, Book 1.

You're Invited!

Immerse yourself in my cozy world!

Find my books, cozy scented candles, tea mugs, and more in my cozy mystery shop.

Nyx Cozy Mystery Shop at www.nyx-halliwell-shop.fourth wall.com/

Free shipping on orders over $30. Discount automatically applied at checkout. Spend $100 and get $20 off!

Ready for more magick?

Don't miss the next exciting adventure! Sign up for Nyx's Cozy Clues Mystery Newsletter at www.nyxhalliwell.com,

And check out these magical stories:

Sister Witches Of Raven Falls Mystery Series
Sister Witches of Raven Falls Special Collection
Of Potions and Portents
Of Curses and Charms
Of Stars and Spells
Of Spirits and Superstition
Sister Witches of Raven Falls Special Collection

Confessions of a Closet Medium Cozy Mystery Series
Confessions of a Closet Medium Special Collection
Pumpkins & Poltergeists
Magic & Mistletoe
Hearts & Haunts
Vows & Vengeance

Cupcakes & Corpses
Tea Leaves & Troubled Spirits
Haunted Honeymoon
Wedding Bells & Psychic Spells
Phantoms Are Forever
Skeletons & Scandals (coming fall 2025)

Confessions of a Closet Medium Cozy Mystery Series

Sister Witches of Story Cove (Formerly Once Upon a Witch) Cozy Mystery Series

Cinder
Belle
Snow
Ruby
Zelle

Sister Witches of Story Cove Complete Set

Witchy Candy Shop Mysteries

Tricks and Treats
Candy and Creeps
Gum and Ghouls

Meet Nyx

USA Today bestselling author Nyx Halliwell loves writing magical stories as much as she loves baking and crafting. She believes cats really can talk (please don't tell her three rescue puppies), and yes, she sees ghosts.

She enjoys binge-watching mystery and paranormal shows with her hubby and reading all types of stories involving magic. She talks to trees, has too many crystals, and drinks far too much tea.

Check out her online store and sign up for her Cozy Corner newsletter at www.nyxhalliwell.com

Dear Magical Reader

Thank you for reading this story! It is an honor and a privilege to write books for you. I'm an indie author and every fan is important to me. I pour my heart into each story and do my best to bring you a delightful escape from the real world.

Readers are the key to my success. Those of you who share my stories with your friends are magic for me.

If you'd like to learn more about my books, sales, and special promotions, please sign up for my newsletter at www.nyxhalliwell.com.

Support me directly (no retailer taking their cut), grab special edition box sets, and get new releases before they are out at retailers by visiting my store. I have sales and offer NEW RELEASES early! Check it out.

Thank you for supporting my dream.

Blessed be,

Nyx 🤍

www.ingramcontent.com/pod-product-compliance
Lightning Source LLC
Chambersburg PA
CBHW021425200626
46814CB00015B/1355